BREAKER

HEARTBREAKERS MC: BOOK 1

ALEXIS ABBOTT

Get an EXCLUSIVE book, **FREE** just as a thank you for signing up for my newsletter! Plus you'll never miss a new release, cover reveal, or promotion!

http://alexisabbott.com/newsletter

PROLOGUE

My eyelids flutter open as a shaft of yellowish light filters across the room and floods over my face. My head is aching, almost pulsing with a dull pain.

What happened?

What did I eat?

Do I have food poisoning?

Am I even awake or is this just a startlingly life-like dream?

Why does this entire room feel like it's rocking back and forth?

I blink rapidly, squinting against the light as my eyes slowly adjust and parts of the room surrounding me begin to come into focus. Maybe I should sit up. Maybe that would make the world stop tilting.

I lick my dry, chapped lips as I try to heave my body upright, but I feel my stomach lurch uncomfortably and I give up for the time being. Looks like I will have to remain horizontal for a minute or so.

My left arm is tingling and prickling underneath me and I realize slowly that my check is pressed against a stained, threadbare pillow case. I fell asleep on my stomach, evidently, but that doesn't make much sense. I hate lying on my stomach and usually I tend to be a side-sleeper, so I must have been awfully exhausted to drift off in this position.

Even though my left arm stings as it comes back to life, I'm able to prop myself up slightly with my right arm.

I wrinkle my nose.

It smells weird in here. That's another irregularity that stands out even though my mind is moving along at a sluggish pace. My bedroom in my parents' house, still frilly pink and filled with stuffed animals I can't bear to part with yet even though I'm eighteen now and presumably a grown-up, always smells like vanilla or patchouli. It's kind of a personal quirk of mine—every evening when I'm doing homework or getting ready for bed, I light one of my many scented candles to set the ambiance in my space. The flickering flame and potent fragrance automatically puts my tension to rest and my body at ease. My candle-collecting is so well known in my friend circle that it's pretty much the guaranteed Christmas or birthday present everyone chooses to give me.

I take my scents very seriously.

But this room doesn't smell like vanilla or patchouli.

It doesn't smell like home.

In fact, it smells like old laundry and stale take-out, made worse by the fact that someone obviously has never cracked a window in this place before. It's like all the bad smells and bad vibes are trapped in this room with me.

My left arm tingles awake and I grunt, dragging myself to sit up with my shoulders against the wobbly metal headboard of the bed. I look around me, taking care to only turn my head slowly. Everything is still spinning slightly, as though I'm trying to look at the world through several sets of bifocals. Or maybe a kaleidoscope like the one I bought at a museum gift shop when I was a little girl.

"Ugh," I murmur, laying a hand on my gurgly stomach. I feel nauseated and dizzy in a way I've never felt before. It's far worse than the time I got the flu during final exams. It's even worse than when my best friend Moxie convinced me to get on that spinny teacup ride at the county fair last year.

Oh, Moxie.

The memories of last night come trickling back

to me like grains of sand through a sieve. My best friend, dancing and laughing under the neon lights. Bright pink and blue flashing across her face. Her cheeks flushed and the blonde curls that frame her face bouncing and slightly damp with sweat.

We go all out when we go out.

Moxie's mom works from home so there's always a parent around, watching us, but at my house there's almost always nobody home. Nobody to tell us to dress more modestly. Nobody to stop us from staying out too late or talking to boys. I guess that's one benefit of being a latchkey kid. Maybe the only benefit.

I can hardly remember how the night began, much less how it ended.

Where the hell is Moxie?

How did I end up in this weird, smelly room?

Who brought me here?

Suddenly, I gasp with fear and peel the bedsheets away from my body. I heave a sigh of relief when I see that I'm still wearing all my clothes, even my tights. Not the most comfortable outfit to sleep in, for sure, but at least it probably means that whoever brought me to this room didn't take all my clothes off. I reach up and tug the stretched-out elastic from my long, wavy auburn hair. I shake my head slightly to fluff out my tangled hair, but I quickly stop and close my eyes tightly against the wave of increased nausea that follows.

"What did I drink last night?" I grumble to myself.

Through the cloudiness in my mind, another question arises: where's my phone?

Come to mention it, where is my purse?

I feel around in the bed and come up with nothing, and when I try to pull myself out of the bed I almost fall over in a heap, my legs buckling underneath me. I hastily clamber back into the bed, pulling my knees up to my chest. I shut my eyes as the room tilts wildly.

Holy cow, I feel like hell warmed over.

I wonder if I got any actual sleep last night. Sure doesn't feel that way, judging from the dull ache in my bones and the fact that I can't stop yawning.

I don't even know what time it is, since the digital alarm clock on the bedside table is flashing midnight. Clearly it got reset during a power outage —which are fairly frequent in my small hometown of Stonedale, Wyoming—and the owner just never got around to setting it back. I can't imagine doing that. At home, I am very particular about everything being in its correct place and in working order. Moxie always teases me about it, because she's the total opposite.

Again, it occurs to me that I have no idea how I ended up separated from her last night. I wrack my brain, trying to piece together the little flashes of incongruent memory I can conjure up from our night out. It started much the way it always did: the two of us jamming to music in my bedroom while we dug through my closet, putting together flirty outfits and doing each other's makeup. Moxie does an incredible smoky eye, while I have the perfect steady hand for winged eyeliner. With our powers combined, we can pull off one hell of a great look.

Another image floats to the forefront of my brain. The two of us dancing to a 'getting ready' playlist while my older sister banged on the wall to get us to turn the music down a notch. I'm the middle child, smack dab in between two older sisters, Leah and Samantha, and two younger brothers, Caleb and Trevor. My little brothers are twins, so they share a room, but we three girls each have our own rooms. Needless to say, my parents have their hands full, but I've always done my best to make it easy on them. I tend to be the problem-solver in my household, the diplomat who works out the conflicts and smooths things over.

I'm a good girl.

Sure, I may not be a genius like Samantha or a saint like Leah. I get average grades, but I rarely miss an assignment. I'm not going to a university, but I do plan to go to the local community college to further my education and get a decent job.

A memory resurfaces out of the fog. Moxie bargaining with a bouncer to let me into a club even though I'm under twenty-one. She leaned on his arm and batted her eyelashes but he wouldn't change his mind. I can perfectly recall the way he shook his head and refused to smile.

Moxie is usually very persuasive. She can talk her way into or out of just about anything, a skill I have always admired from afar. I find it difficult to stand up for myself sometimes, much less talk myself up. But Moxie is different. Her name suits her perfectly, a fact which amuses the both of us to no end. It does mean, however, that she can be a little stubborn from time to time, and last night was the same old story. She argued with that bouncer for a good ten minutes while I stood forlornly off to the side, watching the twenty-somethings easily pass through the doorway into the dimly-lit club with the pulsing loud music.

I remember why we were there in the first place: Moxie was supposed to meet up with this guy she met on a dating app, and she brought me along so I could chat with the guy's friend. Typical double date, only they could all into the club and I am still too young.

I can recall how disappointed and annoyed Moxie was, the way her impish smile turned upside down as she gave up trying to cajole the bouncer. She stepped out of the line and linked her arm with mine. Her eyes flashed light blue in the neon glow of the marquee as she leaned in close to my ear and whispered something.

Oh, what was it?

The words echo in my head.

"Never mind. We'll go somewhere else," she murmured. She sounded exasperated.

What happened next, though? I pinch the bridge of my nose, searching my brain for the next piece of the jigsaw puzzle. The answer stumbled to the stage in the form of a tall, handsome, well-dressed stranger with a smirk that could melt gold. He followed us out of the line of people waiting to get into the club, putting a hand on the small of my back.

"Tough luck with that bouncer, huh?" I remember him saying.

"Yeah, what a jerk," Moxie agreed petulantly.

"Don't worry. I know a place where they'll let you both in, no problem," said the handsome stranger.

I recall the way my heart began to pound, how my hands got all sweaty and clammy. I'm not used to attention from older guys like that. I only recently graduated high school, and I've known the same boys ever since I started preschool. In a small town, that tends to happen. Apart from the rare crush that never lasts long, I haven't dated much at all. Moxie is far more experienced than I am, though, so I turned to her for guidance when that guy came up to talk to us outside the club.

Moxie's mischievous grin burns brightly in my mind. She took the guy's arm and nodded. He led us away from the club. We got into a taxi. I don't remember how long the ride was or where exactly we ended up, only that I didn't recognize that part of town. The whole way there, Moxie flirted with our mysterious new friend, leaning into his space and giggling at his every dumb joke. I remember now— by that point I was already tired. Watching my best friend argue passionately with the bouncer on my behalf was more than enough excitement for one evening, and I had a bad feeling in my gut.

I just wanted to go home, but I stuck around, thinking that I needed to stay and watch over my friend. After all, she had been tossing back shots, pregaming from my parents' liquor cabinet.

I, on the other hand, was stone cold sober. And exhausted.

We walked up to a rough-looking biker bar. From my sheltered perspective, the place might as well have been Sodom or Gomorrah. There were strippers. There were men in leather vests. There were guys arguing at the bar and getting overly competitive at the pool table. The juke box blared the kind of hard rock and roll my parents never played on the radio.

Moxie said we would only stay for one drink.

I believed her.

But one drink turned into two, which snowballed into three. Since I'm only eighteen, I just sipped my cranberry juice like a good girl. Eventually, I got up to go to the bathroom. When I came back to the bar, my stomach flipped. Moxie was nowhere in sight. Neither was her handsome new friend. I vaguely remember trying to call her multiple times, and I never got an answer.

She had abandoned me, which was totally out of character for her.

I must have looked scared, because a guy at the bar pulled me aside and mentioned that he saw Moxie leaving with the man. He also told me that he saw the man put something in her drink. His face swims in my head, annoyingly blurred out. I wish I could remember. Oh, if only I could remember…

The next thing I recall, I was on the back of his motorcycle, the wind whipping through my hair. That's why I pulled it into a ponytail. But it was hard to do. I was uncoordinated, my hands unusually shaky. I felt sleepy, like my thoughts were all slowed down to a near-halt. I couldn't say no. I couldn't even make sense of what was happening around me.

But all I drank was cranberry juice. What in the world could have affected me so strongly?

"Unless…" I mumble.

Unless.

Unless he drugged me.

No. Of course not. That only happens in movies, right?

What are the chances that both Moxie and I were targeted by two separate guys in the same night? It seems impossible. Especially in a small town like Stonedale. Everyone knows everyone. Who would do such a thing?

I assure myself that the man just wanted to help. That he took me back to this place—his place—because I was sleepy and alone and he wanted to save me.

The nausea is starting to go away, thank god. I drag myself out from under the sheets, taking one heavy, plodding step at a time until I cross the shadowy room. I grab the doorknob and try to turn it, but to my confusion, it doesn't turn. I try it over and over again, but it dawns on me gradually that the door is locked… from the other side.

Did that guy really lock me in here? Why would he do that?

Panic floods through my veins, and I'm so on edge that I let out a little yelp of fear when I hear a crackle of thunder outside. I dizzily wobble over to the window, blinking to try and focus my eyes. To my complete surprise, the world I see outside the window is not what I expect. Instead of the rolling green plains of Stonedale, I can make out the dry, cracked brown earth. The sky above is a dark gray, the clouds gathered ominously. I see lightning rumble across the sky.

It could be day. It could be night. I'm not sure. All I know is that this place is not familiar to me.

This is not Stonedale. This is not my home.

"Where the hell am I?" I wonder aloud.

Suddenly, a deafening crash of thunder erupts, making me fall back with fear. In fact, it hardly even sounds like thunder.

It sounds more like a gunshot.

KATE

ears sting in my eyes as I claw uselessly at the wooden window sill. There's a thick block covering up where the access should be, and it's hammered in place with several of those long, sharp nails. I press my palms against the glass and immediately it clouds up with the humidity from my clammy hands. I grunt as I try my hardest to press it up and slide it open, despite the fact that I know full well that pane isn't going to budge. Not when the whole contraption is nailed down like this.

But I can't stop fiddling with it, the feeling of desperation and fear building up in my gut and adding to the cocktail of dizziness, disorientation, and nausea that are already plaguing my confused, weakened body.

I wonder if I can somehow break through the window. Maybe I can take that stupid, flashing alarm clock from the nightstand and bash it through the window pane. It's raining heavily outside now, the clouds gathered thick and dark in the sky, blotting out any semblance of sunshine and making it even more difficult to assume what time it is currently. I bite my lip, eyeing the alarm clock. Do I really have the raw strength and dexterity to successfully slam a small plastic alarm clock through a thick double pane of glass?

I don't have to ruminate for long to determine the answer is no. Besides, there's almost no chance that the window pane would shatter the way I want it to. In fact, I would probably only succeed in shattering the clock and risk hurting my hand.

My mind plays through the scenario over and over again, trying to figure out any possible maneuver that might result in a broken window. But I know, deep in my gut, that it wouldn't work out that way, no matter how desperately I wish for it to happen as I imagine it.

Things in real life almost never pan out the way they would in movies and television. I may be a little young and naive, but even I am not childish enough not to know that.

Even with the cloudiness in my brain, that much is clear to me.

Besides, even if I was to get that window open, I still don't know where the hell I am right now. All I can tell is that I'm not close to home. The world outside the window is alien to me. Instead of the green, lush, idyllic plains of Stonedale, it looks more like a desert of sorts. Dry, cracked earth turning to sticky mud under the pouring rain. Not a tree in sight. Not another house in sight, either.

Stonedale is rural enough on its own, but you still almost always have a neighbor within easy walking distance. It's not country enough to be totally isolated like this place seems to be. If I were to bust through this window somehow, miraculously, I would still just be a lost, physically weakened girl in a foreign place. I don't have my phone. I don't have my wallet.

I can picture it now: me, walking for hours and hours across the desolate landscape without ever running into another living soul who could rescue me from this hell I've landed in.

No.

There's no point in messing with the window anymore.

I still feel as though someone must have slipped something into my drink. It just doesn't make sense otherwise. I know for a fact I was not consuming alcohol on purpose last night. I may be a little braver, a little more reckless when Moxie is around to boost me up with her own devil-may-care attitude, but at the end of the day, I'm still only eighteen years old. I can't order a boozy drink at a bar. I can put on makeup and dress like a grown-up all I want, but I don't have a fake ID. I don't have the smoothness or the lack of conscience to be a successful liar. No matter how tired and distracted I might have been last night, there's no way I would have ordered anything other than my usual cranberry juice.

How in the world would I have managed to score anything else in the first place?

With my soft, youthful face and skinny teen-girl body, I can't successfully pull off the whole 'twenty-something who just happened to forget her ID at home' ruse that Moxie is always pushing me to try. So, if I did somehow imbibe alcohol, it's not because I sought it out myself.

It's because somebody else gave it to me without my even realizing it.

I step back from the window when I realize that I've managed to snap the tips of my glittery-pink fingernails with my attempts to pry it open. I look down sadly at my chipped and broken nails, my heart sinking. Whoever nailed that window down made damn sure a girl like me couldn't rip it open again. It's intentional.

Not just intentional

Planned.

Someone has clearly thought long and hard about the best way to keep a girl like me trapped in a room with no escape. The door is locked from the outside. The window is nailed shut. I have no phone, no way of connecting with the outside world. I'm a fish in a bowl, a bird in a cage. I only wish I knew why someone wants to keep me here like this. Am I someone's shiny new pet? Am I in trouble?

Am I ever going to get out of here?

With the dizziness finally starting to subside enough to let me walk around without falling over, I begin examining the room in deeper detail. I brace myself against the wall with one outstretched arm as I slowly, carefully pace the perimeter of the room. It's messy, but not crowded. Whoever designed this place clearly didn't put too much effort into the design aspect. I'm not dealing with a Feng Shui expert here.

The room doesn't contain a lot of items. The only furniture is the bed, which is just a lumpy old mattress and some stale sheets on a metal bed frame, and a three-legged chair in the corner. I wander over to the chair and give it a nudge with my foot. It falls over with a clattering noise that makes me stumble back and gasp. Evidently, this chair is not suitable for sitting in. So that means the only usable furniture is the bed. I scan the room for more information that might give me an idea of who it all belongs to and why I ended up here. The floor is bare carpet, that typical beige stuff that's cheap and meant to withstand a lot of abuse. It's certainly not stain-resistant, as indicated by the numerous stains of varying colors and shapes and sizes on the floor.

To my horror, one of the stains looks to be a deep, rusty reddish-brown color.

Could that be blood? Or just some weird food stain?

I try to tell myself it's more likely to be something stupid and mundane like barbecue sauce than something dramatic like blood, but then again… the window is nailed shut and I'm locked in here like a prisoner. Obviously, the guy who brought me here isn't a stranger to illicit activities.

I can't believe there was ever a time when I craved being able to live a life like that. Moxie and I can get ourselves into a tight spot from time to time, but never anything truly life-threatening. We stay out too late. We don't always get enough sleep. Sometimes we talk to boys we don't know.

But we don't drink to excess and go home with random guys from grown-up biker bars.

Well, maybe Moxie does.

But I sure as hell don't. I'm annoyed with myself even now, thinking about a conversation I had with Moxie the other day about how boring my life has become, about how desperately I wanted some adventure and excitement in my world. I remember telling her that I needed something new. A new place to explore. A new face other than the usual ones I've been staring at my whole life in my insular community of Stonedale. I was itching for something out of the ordinary.

God, how I wish I could take all that back now. I wanted excitement, sure, but not like this.

I don't know what I was asking the universe for. I get it now, though. I was a fool to think I could find adventure without risk. Excitement without consequences. After all, that's what my parents have always taught me: that stepping outside the lines only puts you in danger, and that it's safer to stay within the neat confines of the rules they've laid out for my siblings and me.

I should have listened to reason. I should have stayed within the rules. I should have colored within the lines. I want to smack myself for daring to branch out. The worst part of it is that I knew, even when I was in the midst of the situation last night, that it was wrong. I had a bad feeling in my gut at the bar. I had a sneaking suspicion that the man who flirted with my friend wasn't completely trustworthy. Hell, I even suspected that the guy who claimed to want to help me was acting with ulterior motives.

And yet I still went through with it all anyway.

That's the part that really stings. I knew I was making a mistake, but I didn't stop myself from making it. I must be the dumbest girl to ever walk this earth. I should have listened to my parents.

Oh, my parents. My heart aches as I imagine them all getting up for church this morning, the one part of the week when my whole family has a chance to spend time together. My mom and dad work constantly, with multiple jobs, to keep us all fed and clothed and keep the bills paid. Sundays are the one day they both take off every week so that we can all go to church together as a cohesive family unit. We get all dressed up. My sisters and I curl our hair. My little brothers wear matching dress clothes. My dad wears a tie. My mom puts on makeup for once—she's a nurse at a local hospital, so she usually couldn't care less about makeup or dressing nicely. In her own words: "I'm just going to end up covered in someone else's bodily fluids anyway."

Again, I feel tears burning in my eyes. I miss them already.

I'm sure they're all worried sick about me. Most days, they're all too busy to notice whether I'm around or not. But Sundays are special. They will most definitely notice that I'm missing. I was supposed to go to church with them. I was supposed to spend time with them, the only chance I get in a week to bond with my parents. With five children in the family, the middle child tends to get left out a lot. But they'll notice I'm not there. It'll be obvious to them.

I hate knowing that I've let them all down. Right now, I'm supposed to be in a church pew wearing my best dress, with my hair in ringlets and just the faintest, softest makeup adorning my face. But instead I'm stuck here in no-man's land, far away from everything I know and love.

There's already tension in my family. I just graduated high school a few months ago, and I'm due to start community college in the swiftly-approaching autumn semester. More than that, though, I'm planning to move out of my parents' house and live on my own for the first time ever. Even though the community college is within commuting distance of home, I have been craving the independence of living in my own place. I have been ravenously searching the internet for affordable apartments, places I could really make my own. It's been one of the most important goals in my mind. My parents, however, think I should stay home with them. They don't think I'm ready to live by myself. So, there's been a lot of stress and misunderstanding in my household lately. Maybe they won't immediately jump to the idea that someone has taken me and stashed me away against my will. Maybe they will just assume I'm acting out, intentionally worrying them to prove a point.

Are they even looking for me?

And on top of that, I still have no idea where my best friend is. Moxie disappeared from the bar when I slipped away to the bathroom, and I haven't seen hide or hair from her since. I can't shake the feeling that I have let her down, too. I should have been there to keep an eye on her. I should have forced her to go to the bar bathroom with me. I never should have let her be alone with that guy, even for five minutes. I wonder where she is, what happened to her. Did she simply have a fun, exciting time with that mystery guy and then take a taxi home safely? Or is she like me, locked up in some room somewhere, terrified and confused?

Swallowing back the lump of terror in my throat, I make my way back over to the window, peering out into the rainy, stormy landscape. This room might as well be a cell. Apart from the bed and the broken chair and the nightstand holding the malfunctioning alarm clock, there are no personal effects. I doubt this is where someone lives full-time. Maybe it's not even a room in a house. Judging from the way the wind is howling around the place, this room feels more like a free-standing structure. Or maybe it's attached to the house, but separate somehow. Like a converted garage. That might explain the lack of personal touches if it's just a second-thought addition to a house. I stare out the window, squinting in search of anything that might help identify where I'm located. Again, I can't seem to find anything familiar out there. No landmarks, no street signs. Nothing.

Wait. Not nothing.

"What is that?" I mumble nervously to myself, leaning closer to the pane.

I hear the rumble of the motorcycle engine long before the image comes close enough for me to really look at it. My heart begins to pound. This is the first sign of life I have noticed all day long. There's a man riding his motorbike out there, and he's getting closer and closer! Remembering that I rode on the back of a motorcycle at some point last night, I try to determine if this is the same guy, but I realize that he doesn't look familiar. He's a different biker, not the one who presumably brought me here.

I gaze at him with wonder. Despite the fact that it's pouring down rain and the dirt roads are all muddy and messed-up, he looks cool and confident, like he's utterly unfazed by the inclement weather. He's close enough now for me to notice that he is also stunningly, shockingly attractive. Even through the heavy rain I can make out his powerful, well-defined jawline and the sharp cut of his cheekbones. He looks like a tall, broad-chested guy—the kind who would easily find work as an athlete or a bouncer or something. As he rides closer and closer, I find myself totally enraptured by his looks. I'm fascinated by him, and I want to know more.

But he doesn't seem to notice me at all. He's clueless, riding along without a care in the world.

What if he can help me? I want to trust him.

Then again, I trusted that guy last night from the biker bar, too, and look where that landed me.

Still, I can't shake the feeling that this guy is different, that he might be my best chance at escaping this stale-smelling cell. So, I decide to start banging on the glass and yelling at the top of my lungs, trying desperately to get his attention as the mysterious hottie rides past, close enough now for me to see the faint shadow of stubble on his face. I beat my fists against the glass and scream until I'm hoarse, but to my dismay he doesn't seem to notice me.

At first.

Thunder rolls over the valley, drowning out my screams. But then, out of the darkness comes a shining light of hope. The biker guy slows down, a look of interest on his handsome face. He turns his head and a shock of electricity shudders down my spine as his eyes lock with mine through the pouring rain.

My heart stops for a moment.

He sees me, and I am known.

Rain patters against my leather jacket and runs down my face in thin streams, but I can't tear my eyes away from the face in the window of the shed. It's hard to make out in the overcast, rainy skies, but I could swear it's a girl. I'm not close enough to tell, but she looks like a pretty little thing, too.

Maybe Roadster's finally bringing someone home? His bike is the only one already here, after all. An overnight stay in the shed sure isn't my idea of romance, but Roadster always did like making girls feel like they were living on the edge.

Or trying to, more like. But last night was Saturday, and the timeline adds up. It's about an hour after noon, not too long after I'd be waking up if I was out with a girl all night and decided to bring her back to my motorcycle club's place.

For a groupie, she looks cute from here. She has the kind of face I wouldn't mind getting a closer look at, if this were an ordinary night out on the town. It looks soft, and there's something innocent to it that you don't see much in the crowd I ride with. That kind of girl would be hard to keep my hands off.

She wouldn't be the first prim, good-girl groupie I loosened up. They call me Heartbreaker for a reason, even if I consider myself on break from earning that nickname.

All that aside, it looks like my buddy finally found himself a groupie down to party, and I have to feel glad for the guy. Credit where credit is due, that looks like a catch in there.

But the longer I stare, the closer I get... something looks wrong. I narrow my eyes as I slow my bike down, and I see that angelic face moving around in the window, followed by a small fist pounding on the glass. Her expression is twisted up, and she isn't looking out in pure curiosity. She's shouting and banging on the glass, and if I didn't know better, I'd think she looks downright terrified.

That doesn't track, for Roadster.

I bring my motorcycle to a slow stop next to his in the still-small row of bikes outside the old warehouse we use as a meeting place for our club. Killing the engine, I swing my leg off and march across the gravel on heavy footsteps toward the front door. I fling it open, and I step into the familiar feelings of the closest thing I have to a home right now.

The interior is still obviously a warehouse, but it is one we've made our own. The ceiling is all exposed infrastructure, vents, and the faint light filtering through usually dirty windows that was streaked with rain from outside. The floor is plain concrete, because our dusty boots don't need anything fancier and it was easier for Eli to clean spilled beer off of. Eli himself stands behind the bar, the only man around anywhere near here who doesn't ride with us.

The bar itself is modest and industrial, too, but the drinks behind it are strong enough to knock any one of us on our ass as often as we wanted. After a long ride, or a longer day taking care of club business, that was hard to beat. A few spartan wooden tables and chairs sit around the warehouse, a pool table taking up the southeast corner next to an old jukebox, and a few other odds and ends we'd brought back to the club to make it look like our own.

There's a large blackboard Eli had hung up behind him, originally to write down new beers or liquors he'd gotten in, but it has proven good for other uses over time, by various hands, judging by the different notes jotted down in every available space:

Bones owes Big Daddy $40. Signed: Bones, Big Daddy, Buzz.

Ironside saved Roadster's ass - 2/16/2013

Breaker kicked Roadster's ass @ pool table - 5/5/2013

Bones owes Roadster $30. Signed: Bones, Roadster, Buzz.

STOP BREAKING POOL STICKS. Signed: Buzz

It's our club's growing piece of history, so over time, we've been finding it harder to erase old things to make room for new ones. That, and Bones's habit of losing bets in pool meant his debts would be up there for us to chuckle at for a while yet.

I give Eli a nod as I approach, and the balding guy with a gruff yet friendly face looks up at me from the TV he was watching on the bar with a smile.

"What's going on, man?" I greet him, leaning against the bar.

"You're early," Eli says.

"Guess I'm the only one who doesn't mind a ride through the rain," I joke with a wink. I was usually the last person to show up to our Sunday meetings. "'Cept Roadster. Seen him around? His bike's outside."

"Think he went out back last I saw him," Eli says. "People been scarce today. Most of them still are sleeping off last night."

"I bet," I chuckle, tapping a knuckle on the bar a couple of times. "Hope they didn't give you too much trouble."

"Nah, I'm just glad Bones put that frat kid on his ass before he could really start trouble," he grunts.

"Damn, should have hung around longer," I mused, and I head past the bar toward the back, giving Eli another nod. "Anyone else shows up, tell 'em I'm dragging Roadster's ass back in here."

"You got it, boss," Eli says absently as he goes back to cleaning glasses.

I step onto the deck out back that overlooks a scenic ditch in the ground, but there's no sign of Roadster until I hear a toilet flushing somewhere behind me. The bathroom door just inside the exit swings open, and Roadster emerges, drying his hands on a paper towel and raising an eyebrow at me.

"Breaker's already here? How long was I in there?" Roadster jokes, and immediately, I punch him on the arm as we break out laughing, and he hits back.

Roadster might be the son of Buzz—our club's prez—but it doesn't mean he's some spoiled brat. In fact, Roadster earns his keep around here and then some, if you ask me. Then again, we are buddies, so we always have each other's back. I'd certainly had Roadster's in more than our share of bar fights, and he had mine. Despite both of us being just shy of twenty-three, we have a few scars to prove it, too.

"Prez here yet? Or anyone?" Roadster asks once

we finished greeting each other and headed back toward the bar together.

"No, I was just looking for you," I say, glancing over at him. "To congratulate you."

Roadster arches an eyebrow.

"What for? I mean, unless you want to cede the pool tournament next month early, in which case, I humbly accept," he grins, putting his hand to his chest in mock grace.

"Fuck you," I grunt, elbowing him with a laugh. "No, I mean the girl, man! You get lucky last night?"

Roadster screws up his face and looks confused. "The fuck you talking about?"

I stare, and gears started turning in my head. "The girl in the shed. I saw her on the way in."

"Sure you didn't have too much to drink last night?" Roadster asks as we sidle up at the bar, and Eli starts getting our drinks ready before we even have to ask. "I got no idea what you're talking about."

I'm starting to get annoyed. "Well, someone's got a friend out in the shed out back, and she didn't look too happy about being there."

"I'll see what Buzz thinks when he gets here, I'm sure he's ahead of us, whatever that's all about," Roadster says with a dismissive wave as Eli sets our drinks in front of us. Buzz has been playing up "big plans" for the past week and even hinted at a big job coming up at the meeting last week, so we're all on the edge of our seats to figure out what's on his mind.

I have a neat glass of bourbon, and Roadster has a vodka. Roadster raises his glass to me before I can take a drink. Confused, but playing along, I raise my glass with him and drink.

"What was that for?" I ask after wiping my mouth.

"You're still alive after that heist I heard you were on last night while we were getting our asses trashed," Roadster chuckles. "That's what for, asshole!"

I roll my eyes, but I allow myself a half-smile.

"C'mon, before the others get here, how'd it go?" he asks, grinning.

"It was a bar outside Rawlins," I say, not liking to brag but not minding filling in a friend, either. "Got a tip from a stripper that the owner was some fuck-head who was stiffing the staff on their tips. 'Percentage based tips,' I hear he was calling them," I scoff. "Anyway, I hit the place up, and the story checked out. Had a talk with the owner, we came to a gentleman's agreement, and now I can call myself the proud partial owner of a dive," I explain. "I get half his profits, he pays his staff good. Win-win."

"That gentleman's agreement have anything to do with that stain?" he asks, nodding down to a dark blotch near the cuff of my jeans.

"Damn, that'll be a bitch to wash out," I grumble.

Roadster was right, though. I had to knock out more teeth than I'd been expecting to get the owner to come to the negotiating table, and I reckoned I used a baseball bat more than most business brokers, but only a little more. Fucker was a piece of shit who didn't deserve those teeth, anyway.

"Alright, Robin Hood," Roadster jokes, chuckling. "You sure that girl out back ain't your Maid Marian you made off with?"

I open my mouth to joke back, but the doors open again, and the rest of the gang files in. Buzz leads the group, as it should be. The big old guy is our prez, and he is twice as fierce as his salt and pepper hair and beard makes him look. Roadster is his spitting image, twenty-something years younger.

The huge piece of work we called Big Daddy comes in behind him. That isn't a name he cares for, but he's our enforcer, and he's earned his place around here in blood on more than one occasion. He tends to be quiet, but his mind is always active, and that makes a lot of people think he's slow when he is anything but.

Bones is at his side, with his usual cocky swagger that gets him into trouble. The guy is a year younger than me, and he has an incredible, red-hot energy to him. Let him out of your sight for as second, and he'll get the better of you. Lot of rivals learned that lesson the hard way over the years. We all know the guy's running from something dangerous, but that has never affected how well he works, so he falls in with our band of misfits just fine.

Ironside brings up the rear, those fierce eyes wearing his trademark thousand-yard stare. He's fresh out of the military, and when he first showed up on our doorsteps, that was all we knew about him and all we *needed* to know. Between him and Big Daddy, nobody fucks with us when we wanted to look intimidating.

"Lookit that, I'm late for my own meeting," Buzz says with a gruff chuckle as he steps into the room.

Roadster is already standing up, like he always does, but I take my time in doing the same. Buzz must be a hard dad to impress, because Roadster always seems eager to prove himself to Buzz. I don't envy him, but I honestly don't know if it is better or worse than the string of step-dads I had growing up.

"Alright, Eli, you know the drill," Buzz says as the bartender starts taking out glasses. "Get us a round of beers, and let's get this meeting started. I got big news for you all. Roadster, you come with me for a minute."

Roadster and I exchange glances, but he doesn't hesitate from following his dad out back while the rest of us take seats. Whatever it is, Buzz looks excited about it, and I'm happy to see Roadster visibly relax a little as they round the corner and vanish from sight.

The rest of us pull up chairs around the biggest

spool table in the room and sit down. Within a minute or two, Eli has pints of frosty beers before us as we all exchange greetings, handshakes, and pats on the shoulder while we take seats. We barely have time to start talking before Buzz and Roadster come back, and as they do, Roadster circles around to me and puts a hand on my shoulder, leaning in close to speak quietly.

"Don't worry about the girl, Dad will explain," he says, grinning. "She's Buzz's new groupie, but she's part of a plan. Just watch."

"That's weird," I murmur while the others are distracted by the Prez, who's cracking a joke about the quality of the beer. "Buzz's old lady usually doesn't like new girls staying here."

Roadster shrugs. "I never know what's on my Dad's mind, but just wait, I think this is gonna be big."

I furrow my brow and looked up at him with confusion on my face, but he only winks at me and makes his way to his seat.

Buzz has Roadster on his right and Big Daddy on his left, as the member with the most seniority. I sit between Bones and Ironside, taste of the bourbon still on my lips when I take my first swig of beer.

"Alright, everyone," Buzz says, putting his hands on the table and looking around at us all with that confident smile he always has when he's about to give good news. "I'm calling this meeting to order.

Don't think I've been hyping things up the past week for nothing, so all you fucks better pay attention."

A gruff chuckle goes around the table as the Prez takes a drink of his beer and sits forward. A few of us glance at each other, probably with smartass cracks in mind, but Buzz commands enough respect at the table that nobody is about to interrupt him.

"I'm not a politician with speech writers, so I'll lay this out on the table plain and simple: I bought a bar," he says, and jaws drop around the table, followed by grins.

"Shit, you're kidding me!" Bones speaks up despite himself.

"Damn, I knew things were going well, but not that well," Ironside says with a grim chuckle.

"What's the place?" I ask, just as enthusiastic as the rest.

"Right now, it's a shit hole called Sir Ray's about an hour's ride east of here," Buzz says.

My smile fades.

That's the name of the bar I hit last night.

What the fuck?

I glance at Roadster, who doesn't seem to have noticed, then back to Buzz without showing my thoughts on my face. I nod slowly, crossing my arms on the table and listening carefully. Something's up, and I have a strange feeling. If that lying-ass bar owner ripped me off, I'll take that baseball bat back to his place and negotiate round two.

"But not for long," Buzz says, grinning. "Because with the money we've been pulling down, I'm gonna flip it. It's going to be the best strip club in the county, no skeezy city fucks with their greasy hands involved, everything handled in house. We already got a bartender, and whatever this place will sell for will pay for the renovations on the bar itself. All we need to worry about is the strippers."

A resounding cheer goes up around the table, with applause, and I don't have a choice but to join in, even though my mind is racing.

"Oh, shit, we could have these meetings in the VIP room," Roadster says, and Buzz chuckles at him.

"Yeah, reckon we could, boy," he agrees. "It's about time we get a proper club to call our own, and we'll run it the way we want. This is a payoff that's gonna keep on giving, and it's already a done deal. Held off on giving you all the good news until I knew it was set in stone."

Fuck. That jackass owner pulled the wool over my eyes, no doubt about it. He sold me a bar that was already sold. He's probably three states away by now.

"Should go without saying," Buzz goes on, "that we'll need strippers if we want a strip club, but I don't think any of you will have problems with that part."

"I'd like to humbly volunteer to run interviews, as much as it pains me," Roadster says with mock humility that makes the whole table laugh with him, even Buzz.

"Actually, I have something else in mind for that," Buzz says, casting a meaningful smile around the table that gets us all exchanging curious glances. "We won't be interviewing girls so much as recruiting them. We don't want anyone who's going to give us trouble, and we want *classy* girls, ones that'll give folks around here real reason to drop some serious money."

"And even more reason for them to drop a different kind of money at the motel down the road," Roadster says in a tone that makes my stomach turn as I realize what they're talking about. "We get our pick of the litter of girls passing through, the good people of Wyoming get a few warm beds at night after a show, and we rake in the money, right Prez?"

Prez gives Roadster an affectionate, fatherly chuckle.

"Yep, and I got our first employee right here, ready to help us get the show on the road," he says. "And I expect each and every one of you to pick one out for yourselves and pitch in, understand? I want a little of all our tastes represented, give it some real local flavor."

My face is expressionless, and the rest of the room feels like it's melting around me. I can't believe what I'm hearing. Knocking over bars owned by assholes is one thing, but what Buzz is talking about is a whole 'nother ballpark. I didn't sign up for this. But there's no question about it.

Buzz wants us to start kidnapping girls to pimp out at that bar… and that girl out back is the first victim.

KATE

God, I am so very tired.

I don't know one-hundred percent how long I have been stuck in this smelly, awful little room, but it feels like a million years have passed since I first woke up this morning. The dazed sensation I woke up with has mostly faded away by now, which I thought would be a good thing, but instead it's just left me feeling even more on-edge and terrified now that the intoxicating substance is out of my system.

As it turns out, that drug—whatever it was and whoever slipped it to me—was the only thing keeping the overwhelming rush of fear and hopelessness at bay. Now that it's worn off, all I can feel is dread and emptiness. I have spent hours, maybe days, maybe weeks just pacing around this crappy little cell in circles. I have done everything I could think of to keep my mind from spiraling out of control into the darkness. I have played mind games. Word games I made up just to pass the time. It's a weird self-comforting habit I picked up back when I was still just a little kid.

I was always a fearful child, for some reason, and I was easily spooked. I used to have nightmares about my teddy bears coming alive to attack me, so they always had to sleep in my closet at night instead of in bed with me. Things like that. I don't know why I was so skittish, but that's just the way it was back then for me, I guess. One time, I accidentally managed to watch an entire horror movie from my hiding place in the living room behind the sofa while Leah and Samantha were having a sleepover with their friends. I, being the younger middle child, was not invited to the little party. They were all in middle school, while I was still a third-grader. Just eight years old and totally traumatized by the blood and guts and violence of the movie they were watching together. I was horrified by all of it, and yet I couldn't look away.

Of course, my parents were out that night. Back then, they were both constantly on the night shift, my mom working the moonlight hours as a nurse in the emergency room at the local hospital, and my father pulling the graveyard shift at the one twenty-four-hour filling station in Stonedale. So there was no one around to comfort me, to tell me it was just a dumb slasher movie and that I was totally safe in my home. So instead, I retreated to the comfort of my frilly pink bedroom. I cuddled my favorite doll and snuggled up under the sheets, shutting my eyes tightly to block out any chance of seeing a monster in my bedroom like the murderer from the film. I played a word-association game my reading teacher taught us in school. I would think of a word, any word, and then come up with a synonym for it. I would make a chain of words, leaping from one defi-nition to the next, until I had ended up as far away from the original word and definition as possible.

Maybe it was silly or childish, but it got me through that awful night. So naturally, now that I was in a dangerous, scary situation again, I returned to that little word game. I spent so long alternating between pacing around the room, banging on the door and window, and just lying on the lumpy mattress flat on my back, staring up at the popcorn ceiling and playing word games to pass the time. I tried my hardest to break the glass window. I banged on the door and screamed until my fists were bruised and my throat burned with exertion. I worked up my energy only to deplete it all in useless attempts at breaking free.

I wandered back to the bed and slumped over on my side, curling up in the fetal position. Tears stung in my eyes and burned hot tracks down my cheeks, dripping down the tip of my nose to stain the moth-eaten bed sheets. I simply am not strong enough to break my way out of here. I'm a scrawny teenage girl, and no amount of screeching or pounding on the window will set me free. I want so badly to get out of this room. I miss my family. I miss Moxie. I even miss boring, quiet, claustrophobic Stonedale. I just want to see something other than these bland four walls and the rainy desolation outside the window.

I've memorized every corner, every nook, every imperfection in the room, and then went on to do the same to the closet.

Just like the room itself, the closet was almost completely empty save for a couple of hangers. They weren't even proper wire hangers, though, just those cheap plastic ones. Still, I tried cracking one across the window pane, just in case they were denser than they looked. But no dice. The hanger was the one that cracked, splitting into three jagged pieces of useless plastic. There's no breaking out of here. I'm not strong enough.

I just have to wait.

And that man I saw earlier, the one who went puttering by on his flashy motorcycle, the one whose intense gaze met with mine… he didn't come to save me. He took one look at me and kept moving along. Like I didn't matter. Like he was looking right through me.

So here I am now, curled up on this filthy

mattress, totally sapped of my strength and hope. There's nothing left for me to try now. It's all over. It's just a waiting game now. How long will I be trapped here? How long will I have to wait to hear another living soul's voice or see a fellow human's face again? Am I just going to waste away to nothing, trapped within these four musty walls? Will I ever see my family and friends again or is this... the end?

I sniffle, rubbing at my tearful eyes. I feel totally hopeless. I reach out and pull the largest shattered piece of the plastic hanger close. It may be useless against the window, but it's the closest thing to a weapon I have found yet, and there may come a moment when I need to defend myself. I roll over on my back and stare up at the ceiling, wincing as I feel a strange prickly sharpness against my scalp.

I sit up, confused and rooting around in my tangled hair for the culprit. I dig through the knotted-up blobs of auburn hair and manage to extract a bobby pin I forgot about. I gaze at it in my palm, turning and examining it in the low light. It's shiny and straight with a pointed end. I wonder vaguely to myself if I can find any use for the item. At this point maybe I'm grasping at straws, but a part of me wonders if I can fashion it into a lock pick of some kind.

I've never picked a lock before, since I have never found myself in a predicament that called for it. But I've seen it done in movies before. It can't be that impossible to figure out, right? Clutching the sharpened hanger fragment like it's my only respite, I cross the room and sit down in front of the door. I reach up for the doorknob and wiggle the bobby pin into the lock, finagling it around. I pick and pick and pick but nothing seems to be working. I just can't figure it out. Evidently, it's not just a skill you can bullshit your way through.

Again, the sense of defeat washes over me and I feel even more exhausted than before.

But then… as I'm sitting in front of the door, something else occurs to me through the darkness. A sound. A somewhat familiar one.

Human voices. Male voices, judging by the deepness and the tenor of them. For the first time, I am detecting signs of life beyond these walls. Maybe I'm not as alone and abandoned as I thought I was. My heart begins to pound and adrenaline floods through my veins. I realize that there is, in fact, something on the other side of the door. Cautiously, unsure of what I'm about to overhear, I lean forward and press my ear against the door. I scarcely let myself even breathe as I focus all my attention and energy on listening to the goings-on beyond the door.

The door is obviously made of a very thick, dense material, because the voices I hear are incredibly muffled. It's infuriating being able to hear the voices but not determine what the hell they're actually saying. It sounds as though I'm trying to play the world's most dangerous game of telephone or something. Still, even though I can't exactly identify the words, I can definitely tell that the voices belong to two men who are talking in angry tones. They sound like they're moments away from coming to blows.

I've always been naturally afraid of men raising their voices, so it takes all my willpower to keep listening and not shy away from the door in fear. Neither of the voices sound especially familiar, to my disappointment. Neither of them sounds much like the man who put me on the back of his motorbike last night. These are different men altogether. I wonder who they are, what they're called. I wonder if they're aware that I'm locked up in here. Surely, they would have heard me by now, right?

Unless the room is better-sealed off than I even thought.

Then, my ears seem to adjust to their voices and I manage to make out a few words here and there. I hear one of the men growl something about transporting across state lines, though I have no idea what he's talking about specifically. The other guy answers in a rageful tone, issuing a very determined and solid *no*. I wonder what the hell they're discussing and why they're so pissed off about it.

I imagine it must have something to do with the location of this crappy little room. Maybe I've been carried across state lines somehow. But then again, the second speaker said *no* pretty adamantly, as though he is issuing a command. And that would indicate that I'm still currently in Wyoming, but that the first man is trying to cajole his way into taking me out of state. I am sure I could be wrong about my interpretation of their argument, but then… it's the best explanation I have come up with so far.

I must still be in Wyoming, just in a part of the state I am not familiar with. I haven't exactly done a lot of traveling in my life. With five kids in my household and a shoestring budget, my family vacations have been more like staycations than traveling abroad. I have only rarely stepped out of the bounds of Stonedale, and even then, I only barely left the area, and never for very long. I press my ear against the door even harder and hear what sounds like two pairs of footsteps echoing across the floor. One of the pair of footsteps seems to dissipate slowly, getting quieter and farther away by the second. I determine that one of the arguing men must have walked away.

But which one?

And why?

Then, to my surprise, I hear the other pair of footsteps… and it's getting closer.

I fall back from the door, clutching the sharpened point of plastic hanger, my eyes wide and my heart hammering painfully in my chest. I realize that this may be my only chance to beg for help. I hurriedly get up on my knees and start banging on the door with my free hand, shouting and yelling.

"Help me! Please! Let me out of here!" I wail. "At least bring me some water or food, I'm starving! Help, help!"

The footsteps are so close now, and then they stop short in front of the door. I can feel him there. I can see the faintest shadow underneath the door. He's there. I can hear his breathing.

"Please open the door," I beg. "Let me out!"

The man says nothing. Instead, I'm quieted by the appearance of two small white pills being shoved underneath the door frame into the room. I frown down at them in disgust. There's no marking on them, and I can barely see them in the darkness of the room, but I know one thing for certain: I will not take these mystery pills.

Hell, no.

"I'm not taking any drugs. I want food. Or water!" I demand angrily, shoving the pills back under the door. Before I can say another word, the pills get pushed back to me again.

A gruff voice interrupts me and says, "You can do this the easy way or the hard way. Take the damn pills."

I stare down at the white pills, shocked to hear the man's voice.

"No! You can't make me take these stupid drugs. Let me go," I reply defiantly.

"Look, I am trying to help you," the man hisses between gritted teeth. "But you have to help me, too, little girl."

"What do you mean? How the hell can I help you when I'm locked in this disgusting room? Where is my friend? What did you do to me? Where am I?" I ramble off.

"Keep your voice down," the man orders in a growling undertone.

"No! I need answers," I shoot back.

Silence.

Something in me told me I needed to be silent too.

Next thing I know, I hear rapid, heavy footsteps approaching, as well as a discord of enraged male voices shouting at one another. I hear shoes scuffing on the floor, the sounds of grunting and bones crunching and fists connecting with faces. I clap a hand over my mouth, listening to what sounds like pure carnage on the other side of the door. Bodies slump to the floor. Men cry out in agony and fear. Then there's a deep silence, broken only by a heaving breath. I hold my own breath, waiting to see what has happened beyond the door.

And then, to my shock, the door knob jiggles and the door falls open with an eerie creaking sound. I squint my eyes at the onslaught of bright light flooding into the room as the door opens. A huge man is silhouetted in the doorway, and behind him on the floor is the body of a fallen man. I gasp in horror when I realize he's not moving at all. Around his head, a pool of scarlet blood spreads out like an unholy halo.

He's dead.

And for all I know, I could be next.

BREAKER

I feel the trickle of blood that isn't my own running down from my gleaming brass knuckles I'm still clutching. Its wet warmth runs down my thick fingers and beads up at my fingertips before falling to the ground like a silent witness to what I had just done. The woman before me stares at me with wide eyes full of fear, like an animal trapped by the hunter, trembling like a leaf.

And the only comfort I have to offer isn't going to make her feel much better.

What I did was cross the point of no return, and now, I feel like the midnight stars are gazing down on me with as much shock as the beautiful woman in front of me. She's more beautiful than I could have possibly imagined. The hair I saw framing her delicate features is a rich and soft auburn. Her clothes look a little worn by now, and I can only imagine she's been through a lot, but she still looks so radiant that it seems almost criminal for me to be standing here, staring at her… especially in light of the situation.

That part hasn't quite set in yet, but the fact is there.

I just killed Roadster.

It feels so childish now to tell myself that he started it, but it's true. The rest of the meeting couldn't have been more uncomfortable, but I held it together the whole time, nodding along with whatever the prez said. I was always quiet during meetings, unless I had something important to say, so it didn't seem out of line. Spending the rest of the day with the guys didn't feel right in the slightest, especially because Roadster kept me busy the whole time.

We spent hours shooting pool and discussing plans for the club. I humored him at first, avoiding the elephant in the room while Buzz and the others kept to themselves. I wondered what the other three thought about all this bullshit, but I had no way of knowing. They had been as tight-lipped at the meeting as I had, with a few exceptions. Buzz was a hard man, and he had the club's respect, including mine. Up until now.

But after hours of shooting the breeze about what we might do with the money the place will rake in and how we want the new place to look, we went to get takeout, and Roadster started drinking more heavily the second we got back. He said stupid shit when he drank. He had always been like that. I knew it was only a matter of time before I was forced to deal with one ugly conversation, but I never dreamed it would play out like this.

Half an hour ago, more than a little buzzed, asked me if I wanted to come check out our "down payment" on the bar that Buzz had just bought. The rest of the guys were busy with a poker game, so I followed him, but not because I wanted to ogle the prisoner like he did. I wanted to have a heart to heart with a man I called my friend.

As we stepped out into the cool night sky, he dodged out to take a leak. I had just a second to try to put my plan into action, but there wasn't enough time. She was too frightened to submit.

The second he returned, I realized there was only one option through this. I had to get Roadster on my side. I had to know that he still had a conscience.

"Are you really down with what Buzz is doing, man?" I asked as we started heading around to the shed. "I didn't hear anything about this."

"What are you talking about?" he asked, glancing over his shoulder at me. "Pissed off that my dad snatched the bar out from under your nose? I mean, that's fair, but at least you got to kick someone's ass. So, the night wasn't a total waste, yeah?"

"You know damn well what I'm talking about," I said a little more aggressively, and this time, I picked up the pace so that I could stand side by side with him. He came to a stop, swaying a little, but looking vaguely surprised at me. "The girl," I growled.

"Jesus, dude, we're getting to her, chill," he said, chuckling. "Has it been a while? Figured you'd have gotten laid before coming home last night."

"That's not what I mean, River," I said, taking a step closer. Roadster looked taken aback by my use of his real name, and his warm, fuzzy expression started to go cold.

"Don't tell me you're getting cold feet, Breaker," he said, and the warning undertone in his voice wasn't lost on me. "This ain't the time for that."

"Cold feet?" I said. "You and I have robbed a loan shark at gunpoint in this gang, and we've personally put a pimp six feet under outside Pocatello. This is not us, Roadster. What the fuck is Buzz doing?"

"What my dad is doing, Breaker, is making this club worth something," Roadster snarled, taking a step closer to me. I held my ground. "Unless you want to live out the rest of your sorry-ass life knocking over convenience stores and dive bars, we all need to be on the same page with this."

"I'm not," I said firmly, and the words seemed to hang between us with stunning force for a moment.

We locked eyes, and I could feel my heart trying to pound out of its chest. My fists were tight, and my body was poised. I knew what Roadster looked like when he was about to start swinging, and his body was wound up tight as a spring, ready to go.

"*Think we need to talk to Buzz, Breaker,*" *Roadster said, deadly tension in his tone.*

"*Nah, that's not gonna happen,*" *I said in a slow but clear tone, fully aware of what that meant.* "*I'm going to open that shed, and that girl is going home. Period.*"

I watched Roadster's jaw tighten.

"*Can't let you screw this up, Breaker,*" *he said.* "*Dad's been good to you. I've been good to you. And if you want us to keep being good to you, what you need to do right now is fall in line, even if I've gotta put you there.*"

"*River,*" *I warned him,* "*don't do anything st-*"

Roadster swung at me, and I leaned back just in time to feel his knuckle graze my chin. In an instant, the tension broke, and the world seemed to move ten times as fast. Roadster lunged at me, but I was faster. I grabbed his wrist and pulled him with his own momentum, and I watched him stagger as I got myself ready.

What I hadn't been expecting was him pulling that switchblade.

I cursed and reached into my pocket, slipping the brass knuckles over my fingers and pulling them out so Roadster could see them. But Roadster was seeing red. He must have had more to drink than I realized, or maybe the idea of going against his dad just got under his skin too well. He came in hard and fast, and if I hadn't moved in time, he would have plunged that knife into my gut.

Roadster's inexperience was showing, and it almost cost me my life. Older members wouldn't be fighting to kill, but Roadster always had that damn temper of his. I'd fought with him before, but I knew that look on his face.

When he came at me again, I saw my opening and went for it. One solid blow to the jaw would be all it took, I thought. I'd break it and knock a few teeth out, knock him out if I was lucky. All I needed was enough to put him out of action long enough for me to get the girl and run.

Instead, Roadster staggered on his own attack, and his head came forward a hell of a lot faster than I thought it would. My brass knuckles caught him right on the temple, and I felt them sink in and crack skull.

The moment his body hit the ground, it stunned me. Somehow, I knew. Before I even stooped down to check his pulse, I knew he was gone by the way he fell, even though I couldn't explain it. And indeed, his heart went still as blood poured from the head wound. My face went pale, but I had no time for my conscience to catch up to me. I grabbed the keys off his belt and made for the shed.

And now, I'm standing before the most beautiful woman in the world with fresh blood on my hands.

"Please, I-I don't have anything-" she starts to say, but I shake my head and offer her my hand, which gives her pause.

"No time," I grunt, gesturing for her to hurry up and come out of the shed. "We need to move. I'm getting you out of here, and you're not going to want to stick around for what happens when the others find out about this," I say, holding up my bloodied brass knuckles.

It didn't occur to me until it was too late that brandishing a murder weapon isn't the most comforting thing in the world, but the redhead surprises me by looking relieved and hurrying out of the shed immediately. She doesn't hesitate for a moment… at least, until she sees the body behind me and puts her hands to her mouth.

"Is he…?" she asks, afraid of the answer.

"Honey, we need to *go*," I order more firmly, and I start heading toward the row of bikes.

"Where's Moxie?" she asks as she hurries after me, but I put my finger to my lips as we make our way around the warehouse and get to my bike. My keys are already out, and I finally slip my brass knuckles off in my pocket before getting on and looking to her. I'm half-expecting her to jump on the back without further question, but instead, she's standing a few feet away, looking like her nerves are catching up to her.

"Not the time for second thoughts, kid," I say, shaking my head.

"I-" she stammers, looking back at the warehouse door in terror before looking back at me. "I-I-I don't… what the fuck is even happening?" she breathes, and I can sense panic threatening to grip her. "Where's Moxie? Where's my friend?"

"I honestly have no idea who that is or where

they might be," I say as curtly and urgently as this situation calls for. "But if we want to get out of here alive, you need to listen up: if you don't get on the back of this bike, the guys in there are going to have *you* entertaining scumbags the rest of your life, after they torture me to death. Your call."

"I have no idea who you are," she says, shaking her head quickly, eyes wide and face pale. "I-I don't know where my friend is, or where the hell we are! I'm not going anywhere with you!"

"Keep your voice down," I hiss. "We've still got time on our side, but we've got to get the fuck out of here before someone finds that body. You've been kidnapped, and I'm getting you out. Are you game, or do you want to take your chances with them?"

She looks about as stunned at that as I would expect, and before she can answer, a voice from behind the warehouse gets our attention.

"Roadster, where the fuck did you two get off to?" Buzz calls, and my heart skips a beat.

"Time's up, kid," I growl, firing up my engine. The powerful roar of the engine is a dead giveaway that something is up, and I know it's now a matter of minutes—if not seconds—before the club realizes the truth.

That they have a traitor in their midst, and it's me.

I hoped the engine roar would snap her out of her paralyzed panic and get her to start thinking sensibly, and I'm pleasantly surprised when it seems to work like a charm. She curses and hurries onto the back of the bike, gripping my kutte with her small hands. I catch a whiff of her sweet perfume as I rev the engine and take off, leaving my old life behind me.

The warehouse compound near Table Rock, Wyoming looks abandoned from the outside, besides the fact that it has a working gatehouse and a rusty chain link fence that surrounds the place. When the club moved in, we figured it had been used to store some military equipment or some shit like that. It worked like a charm for us, but now it presented one more hurdle to get through.

I pull my bike up the road toward the gatehouse, where a lone prospect sits watching something on a grainy little television. He stands up as my bike approaches, and I turn to speak to the girl in as quiet a tone as I can manage without letting the prospect hear.

"Play it cool, let me do the talking," I say, and she gives me a squeeze to let me know she understands. I have to admit, I always thought of myself as a lone rider, but the warmth from her body on my back feels nice.

"Hey, Breaker," the prospect says, a skinny young punk nicknamed Skid, leaning out the window and eyeing the girl up and down. She isn't even mine, but I feel a protective instinct rear up in me, and I shoot the guy a glare. He gives me an apologetic smile and scratches the back of his neck. "Heading out for a ride? Thought everyone was in for the night."

"Yeah, last-minute run for the prez," I say curtly, nodding back toward the warehouse. "Gotta be quick though, I hear there are pigs watching the highway tonight."

"Oh, yeah, for sure," Skid says, and he quickly hits the button to open the gate. "Watch your back out there. Want me to-"

Before he can finish his sentence, a light at the warehouse gets our attention, and our eyes snap to the door. Someone just threw it open, and by the looks of the silhouette, it's Buzz. He cups his hands around his mouth and starts to shout something, but before he can get the warning out to Skid, I rev my engine and drown out his voice.

The next second, I fly forward, and the bottom of the gate barely grazes me as I fly through it, hurdling down the road as fast as my bike can accelerate. All at once, I feel the cool, dry night air in my face and the warmth of the girl's arms tight around my torso as we blaze out of the compound to the chaotic sounds behind us.

And through all the voices, the sound of a shotgun blast pierces the night's sky. We're about to have company.

Well, this is shaping up to be the strangest chapter of my life thus far.

I feel as though I have fallen, Alice-like, down some crazy rabbit hole and ended up in a world far beyond the quiet, routine little universe I've been living in all my eighteen years. I have never known this kind of exhilaration, tempered with a healthy edge of fear.

My arms are wrapped tightly around the muscular torso of the most handsome and dangerous-looking man I have ever seen, holding on for dear life while he rockets a speeding hunk of heavy metal and exhaust smoke down a darkened highway under the eerie glow of the moon. I feel like a character from one of those bodice-ripper made-for-television movies my mom likes to watch in secret when we're all asleep at night. (Naturally, I've sneaked peeks of these edgy flicks from behind the sofa over the years—how could I resist?)

All around me, the wind whips through my auburn hair, prickling up goosebumps along my arms and legs. Adrenaline pumps through my veins, making my heart race and my mind ricochet in a million directions. There's just so much to take in, it's almost too much to handle. If I had a free hand, I might actually be tempted to pinch myself. This sure feels more like a crazy dream than any version of reality I've ever run into before.

I can feel every tense, powerful muscle rippling underneath my savior's clothing as he grips the steering bars.

At least, I hope he's my savior. After all, this is much like how my kidnapping began. From what I can remember of it.

The motorbike careens around corners, tilting from side to side and the way that both terrifies and thrills me at the same time. It's all I can do to hold on and keep myself upright on the back of the motorcycle. But the man at the helm seems totally in his element. He's steadfast and strong, and I find myself instantly feeling safer with him so close.

I know how crazy that must be. On some level, I realize that I have no real reason to trust him so completely. After all, as far as I know he's part of the same team of bad guys who locked me up in that smelly old room. Who knows what kind of foul intentions they had in mind for a girl like me? I may be sheltered, but even I'm not naive enough to think their motivations were at all pure and good-hearted.

Maybe they were going to sell me off to the highest bidder.

Maybe they planned to keep me around for… well, their own *purposes*.

I shudder to think what would have become of me if my savior hadn't shown up at that exact moment to spring me free from my prison. Surely, I can trust him, right? If he was a bad guy, he would have left me there in that room. He would not have given my plight a second thought, just moved on with his own life, his own motivations.

But no. He set me free. Of course, those other guys sure don't plan on giving me up without a fight, judging by how fast he has to drive this motorbike to evade capture. What will become of me if they catch up to us? What will my family think? What if I never see the domestic boredom of Stonedale again?

Well, actually, that part doesn't sound so awful, if I'm being perfectly honest. But the point still stands —what will happen to me if my savior decides I'm not worth the trouble? If he's one of them, is he betraying their trust, their camaraderie, just to save me?

Suddenly, the motorcycle swerves around a tight left corner and the bike angles dangerously close to the ground. Stricken with terror, I can't help but let out a little squeal of fear. I hold on more tightly, my fingernails digging into the front of my rescuer's broad chest. I glance back over my shoulder and feel my heart drop down to my stomach.

They're still behind us—and gaining momentum by the looks of it. I turn back and bury my face in the man's back, closing my eyes tightly as though I can block out the world by pretending not to see it. But even with my eyes closed I can still hear the rumble of motor engines behind us, the crunch and grind of tires on muddy, wet dirt roads. I still don't recognize the countryside whirring past us. It might as well be another planet, as far as I can tell. And I'm just as useless and helpless as I would be floating around out in space.

Only I'm not alone. In fact, I have the world's most dangerous man guiding me. I just wish I knew for sure that I can trust him to be the savior I need.

After all, he did offer me drugs. Actually, he kind of pushed them on me. And then there's the whole part where he might just have killed a man. I swallow hard, fear creeping up to sit heavy in my stomach like a stone. I reassure myself with the fact that it's not like I had much of a choice in the matter anyway.

When a man like this one says it's time to go, what chance does a girl like me have to say no?

What could I have said? "No, thanks. I'll take my chances with the other big, scary dudes who drugged me, kidnapped me, and locked me up in a room?"

No.

This is the only way.

I may be exhausted. I may be so desperately hungry that my vision is blurred and my head is aching, but anything is preferable to being cooped up in a filthy room in the middle of no man's land. For better or for worse, I'm with him now. He's my best chance at survival. If I ever want to see my family and friends again, I have to pour all of my trust and promise into him.

I only hope he can outpace the veritable caravan of bad guys hot on our trail. They sure aren't giving up easily. It makes me wonder even more what the hell they want from me. It's not like my family has any money to offer. What could they want me for?

Ransom?

If that's what they are wanting, then they definitely picked the wrong girl. But I have a feeling it must be something much more diabolical than that. Something I don't really want to put too much thought into at the moment. At least not until we're in the clear. Right now, it's just all about survival. Just about escaping the immediate danger hot on our heels.

And with the minutes creeping toward the dark, ominous hours of early morning, our situation seems more and more dire. Where is he taking me?

Where can we possibly go to get away from these men? And when and if we do, what will become of me then?

What will he do with me?

A shiver runs down my spine. I have no way of predicting that. I could beg for my life. I could appeal to his conscience. But if he really rubs elbows with the kind of gang who captured me in the first place, who's to say any of that would make a difference?

"I'm scared," I murmured, half to myself and half to him.

He lets go of the steering grip with one hand and places it over both of my trembling hands. He gives them a gentle squeeze, which strangely does make me feel marginally less terrified. I can feel the goodness, the pure intentions radiating from him like a nightlight in the dark. My heart slows down a little. My shoulders relax slightly, rolling down from the tight hunch I have been frozen in for the entire ride. I can sense he doesn't want to hurt me. Maybe I'm naive. Maybe it's wishful thinking.

But it feels real to me.

His hand over mine, the warmth of his body against me, it's all better than a shot of whiskey for calming the nerves.

So, there's hope yet for a conscience in him.

I choose to believe that.

As if I have any other option.

We barrel down the misty, muggy back roads, lit only by the eerie moonlight and the scattered stars. Out here in the middle of nowhere, it's all too common to drive for hours without seeing a streetlight, much less a stop light or a town. Even the occasional building we drive past looks totally abandoned, as though nobody has taken these roads in ages. I don't see any street signs, and there certainly aren't any street names for me to recognize.

Every now and then I see a leaning, dilapidated shell of a house, but other than that the roads are empty. It's very creepy, like crossing over into some bizarre shadow world. I can't help but wonder where exactly on the wide, empty map of Wyoming we fall right now. How far flung am I from home? Would anyone look here to find me? Wyoming is such a massive, rural state. There are miles and miles of mostly-unchecked, untouched wilderness, and even beyond that the towns are so few and far between we could probably ride for hours without coming across one.

It's easy to feel lonely in a place like this. Even in Stonedale, where I have lived my entire life, it can sometimes feel as though we all live in a tightly-sealed vacuum, far away and cut off from the rest of the world. We are set in our ways there, and rarely does a stranger blow through town to make some noise and shift things up. Change comes very slowly to the quiet corners of the world, and I know without a doubt that Stonedale is one of the quietest.

"Where the hell are we?" I hiss, leaning forward to get my lips as close to his ear as possible. I can feel him shiver slightly, affected by the ticklishness of my breath against his ear.

"It won't matter where we are if we don't shake these guys," he growls back.

"How do we do that?" I ask fearfully. I glance back over my shoulder again, almost too afraid to even look. To my horror, they appear to be gaining on us, the motorcycles kicking up clouds of dust in their hot pursuit.

"Like this," my savior replies in a gruff voice, and before I can give his words a second thought, he revs the engine to a deafening roar, picking up even more speed and careening sharply around a corner.

I scream and hold on as tight as I can, screwing my eyes shut amid the dust and dirt kicked up by the bike tires. The motorcycle leans to the right so far that for a few seconds I am totally certain we're going to tip over. I clench my teeth, preparing for the inevitable tumble. I may not be a rough rider myself, but I am more than aware of how dangerous a bike like this on roads like these can be. I've seen the photos of mangled limbs and full-body burns, scars glistening on the bodies of people who took a turn too quickly and went flying off the bike. I know the risks, and I am sure he does, too. But he doesn't seem to let fear keep him from doing what his instincts tell him to do. He doesn't listen to the little voice that says no, no, no.

He only knows yes, and he's willing to risk everything in pursuit of it.

Normally, that would make him exactly the kind of guy I try to avoid. I like a little mischief sometimes, but never real danger. Except that it's different with him. Don't get me wrong—I'm scared out of my damn mind. But there's something in my heart telling me to trust him. Whatever the reason may be—desperation, fear, even loneliness—I believe in his ability to protect me, and that makes me his for as long as he wants to keep me around.

Especially when I realize that he's starting to shake off our assailants. One by one, they seem to drop back a little and fall out of sight. I steal a look back over my shoulder and I'm surprised to see that the number of people pursuing us has lessened considerably. And that is when, suddenly, everything around me goes totally dark.

I gasp, fearing the worst, until I realize that it's only dark because my savior here has cut off the lights. He's driving in near-total blackness, and yet he seems just as sure of himself as he was before. I feel a roughness underneath us as he veers the motorcycle off the dirt road and over the grass, the engine puttering and whining in protest.

"What are you doing?" I hiss, terrified that we'll lose the advance we've built up.

"Shh," he rumbles back to me.

I open my mouth to protest more, but I stop myself, realizing there's no point in arguing. Clearly, he knows way better than I do what we should be doing right now. What advice do I have to offer a guy like him in a time like this anyway? So I zip my lips and try not to let my heart pound out of my chest as the motorbike slows down. He rolls us along across the dewy grass and cracked earth, hurtling toward a big, looming black shape in the dimness. It looks at first like some massive behemoth rising out of the fog to devour us whole, but it dawns on me slowly that it's actually just an old, worn-out skeleton of a house. My savior keeps the engine rolling, the tires putt-putting over harsh earth until we swerve around behind the shadowy house, and he cuts the engine completely.

The stillness and silence that follows is almost too much to bear. Now that it's deathly quiet, all I can hear are my own labored, fearful breaths. Terror grips every inch of my tensed body as I sit perched on the back of the motorcycle, still clinging to the man in front of me like he's the only floating plank in a shipwreck. I can hear the other bikes rumbling in the distance, but they seem to get louder and louder, getting closer.

"Be quiet," he murmurs, barely loud enough for me to hear.

My breath catches and holds in my throat as I listen to the horrible grinding of the motorcycle engines as they approach. Louder, closer. Louder, even closer. And then... miraculously, the engine gets softer, and I realize with a jolt of amazement that they're passing us by. We have somehow successfully hoodwinked them and hidden away. We really did manage to shake them off the trail. I tremble in the cold and my savior takes my freezing hands between his own, rubbing them rhythmically to warm them back up. I'm almost taken aback by this gesture of kindness, and when he wordlessly offers me his leather jacket, I hardly know how to respond. Luckily, he catches on to my confusion and simply drapes the jacket around my shoulders. I shrug into it thankfully, feeling his scent and warmth wash over me.

Once we can no longer hear any rumble of the motorcycle engines, I dare to speak.

"What... what are you going to do with me?" I mumble, afraid of the answer.

Through the darkness, he fixes me with an intense stare and says, "I haven't decided yet."

I feel the shiver run through her body at my words plain as anything, and I feel a soft smile tug at the corners of my lips. This is the last time to be thinking about the way my words affect this girl's body, but I can't deny that if this were any other situation… it would be hard to keep my hands off her, much less my eyes.

The scent of her behind me, getting all over me, is almost too much to bear. She's had her hands around my waist, and the ends of her hair tickling the base of my neck, and I know she's softer than anyone I've ever touched. She would be so much softer without those clothes on her body.

But I can't let myself get distracted by that.

Minutes pass like hours, and even the occasional rustling of an animal in the distance makes the girl on my back twitch. She's nervous, and the sound of her breathing is nearly silent yet still somehow almost deafening. Even it sounds like music to my ears, but what I'm really listening for is the telltale sound of roaring motorcycles and the voices of the men I used to call my comrades.

Used to.

That's going to take some time to adapt to. When I woke up this morning, I still saw myself twenty years from now with guys from this club, assuming I hadn't taken a belly full of lead by then. But then again, when I got up this morning, I had no way of knowing what Buzz is truly capable of.

And Roadster.

Fuck, Roadster.

I can't think about that right now. What's done is done. My own two hands took a life, and now, they have to save one.

Eventually, I decide that I've successfully lost them, at least enough that I can keep moving. And that's the important part: keep moving until I can find somewhere truly safe. Wyoming is a lot of stretches of long, empty road with not much in between, and that means hiding can be a unique challenge. Fortunately, we bikers have our ways.

The girl nearly jumps when I start rolling us forward again. Her heart had just started to slow down, but it picks right back up as my engine rumbles and the bike carries us back onto the road, into the pale moonlight.

That last question is still hanging over the girl behind me, and as I ride past weathered old buildings and bone-dry earth, I realize just how tightly she's holding on. She's scared. Terrified. How could she be anything but? A day ago, she was getting kidnapped, and now, she might as well be getting kidnapped again.

For all she knows, I could be lying to her. I could be just a gang member who decided to take this captive for myself, ride her out into the desert to whatever fate I wanted to inflict on her. Hell, that's more or less what I'm doing, I just don't have a way to prove that my intentions aren't downright villainous.

I turn my head at the sight of an oddly shaped shadow that turns out to be nothing but a shadowy rock on the side of the highway, but I feel the girl flinch. That makes my heart sink. It's a flinch that I know all too well, and it makes me feel bad as hell that I'm making someone else react that way.

As the arid wind blows over my face and through my hair, my mind carries me back to when I was a kid, watching my mom bringing home boyfriend after boyfriend, each one usually some level of worse than the last. There was anger in their every action. An explosion was behind every word in that tone I knew all too well. It was in their every look, every time they moved their hands, so close to turning to violence.

I watched my mom flinch from them.

Am I the kind of man that women flinch from?

I've been trying to get away from my past as a heartbreaker, but the name still follows me, reminding me of where I'd come from. But I'd never broken another part of a woman's body, and I don't intend to start tonight.

We ride under the pale orange light of a street light that isn't long for this world, and the brief moment of illumination shows me the drying blood on my knuckles—Roadster's blood. My jaw tightens, and I force myself to keep my eyes on the road. I can't let myself get distracted in grief.

Just keep riding forwards.

It's cold tonight, but knowing that the girl has my jacket over her shoulders now makes me feel better about it. Besides, the chill of the wind keeps me awake and alert without freezing me to the core, so it's a welcome evil right now. I need to keep my wits about me. One wrong move, and I'll be faced with a long stretch of empty highway to watch our doom roll toward us on thundering motorcycles. There's not a lot of room for subtlety on bikes like mine. You move smart and careful, not stealthily.

Shame that stealth is the only thing that'll get us through tonight.

She doesn't speak for a while as I ride, and I'm surprised by that. I would have figured she'd at least ask me where we're headed again, but she seems to have taken my last words to heart. Maybe she's too afraid to say anything at all. That thought twists a knife in my gut, and I can't let the silence go on much longer.

I decide to break the ice.

"Hey," I shout over my shoulder, talking over the roar of the bike.

"What?" she shouts back.

"Can you hear me?"

"Kind of!"

I pause for a moment, thinking what the best way to go about this might be.

"What's your name?" I finally ask.

She hesitates.

She doesn't want to give it.

That's reasonable, I decide, but I don't want to be running around with someone I'm just calling "the girl" as long as we're together. Maybe I can get her to open up if I meet her halfway first.

"Call me Breaker," I shout.

"That's what I heard them say," she replies, and I wonder if she really does consider me just 'one of them' and no better. I can't say I can blame her, if she does.

Another pause.

"Kate," she says at last.

"Kate?" I confirm, shouting over my shoulder, and I feel her squeeze me in confirmation. "That's a nice name. You look like a Kate."

"Th… thanks," she says, sounding surprised.

I meant to take her off guard and make her feel a little more comfortable with some lighthearted conversation, and I could swear I feel her relax a little. She doesn't ask for my real name, either, and I'm glad for that. I don't want to lie to her, but I don't want to give away my real name, either.

Is it unfair of me to ask for her name, then? Sure, maybe it is. Then again, Kate could be a fake name too. That part doesn't really matter. I just need something to call her. I'm not the one who's been kidnapped, and if she were to get loose and run to the police immediately, I'd be the first one in hot water.

"Where are you from?" I ask after a few moments of silence.

"Stonedale," she replies, and my eyebrows go up. That's a decent distance from here. "We're… we're not heading in that direction, are we?"

"I can't take you back there, Kate," I shout. "They're going to be looking for both of us. Stonedale is probably the first place they'll be after you, because they don't want you talking to the police."

"I won't, I swear!" she shouts, and I have to feel bad for her. She has no idea how naive her words sound. She can't be a day older than eighteen, so I can hardly blame her for that. "I won't talk to anyone, I just need to find Moxie and get home."

I don't reply to that, because I don't have an answer she'll like. She realizes that after a few seconds of silence, and it breaks my heart to feel the anxiety radiating off her.

Soon, we come up to a small roadside area that doesn't even seem to be a town, just a resting station for truckers and travelers. There are a few gas stations and a ragged old fast food joint, with an eerie light coming from the drive-thru window, but most importantly, there's a motel with a vacancy sign nearby.

I feel Kate's grip tighten on me in anticipation as she realizes that I'm heading toward it. This has been my plan since I left our poor excuse for a hiding spot earlier and hit the road again. I don't know how the hell I'll be able to hide my bike, but I need to get somewhere we can hunker down for the night and rest.

"Are we stopping for the night?" she asks.

"Yeah, I'm getting a room so we can-" I start to say, but I cut myself off halfway through the sentence as I enter the parking lot.

Big Daddy's bike is parked in the lot.

"Fuck!" I curse, and I roar out of the parking lot, going back onto the highway as Kate hugs me tight and stifles a cry of terror. But I know it's too late already. They were waiting for me, and now, there's no chance they don't know I'm here.

But when I want to move, I can move fast.

My engine rumbles under us as I accelerate down the road, speeding along so fast that it stings my eyes bitterly. There's so much highway behind us by the time I hear the distant roars of motorcycles, I feel as safe as I can possibly feel out here.

And that's not saying much.

Kate seems to relax little by little as she realizes the bikers aren't going to catch up with us that easily, but she's still tense as we ride onward, and this time, I don't know how long we'll be riding before we're able to stop… if ever.

"Do you think Moxie is still back at the warehouse?" she shouts.

"There's nobody at the compound besides the club and any groupies hanging out," I shout back. "That's what I thought you were when I first saw you."

"Groupies?" she asks, and I wince.

"People who aren't members or prospects, but they're hanging out willingly," I explain. "Usually to sleep around with us."

"Oh," she says more quietly.

"What does your friend look like?" I ask.

"Curly blonde hair, kind of a party girl, hard to miss," she says, choosing her words carefully over the loud rush of wind.

"Don't remember anyone like that anytime recently," I say, shaking my head. "I'm sorry, but I don't think they have your friend. That might be good news for you both, though."

"No, yeah, that's… that's good, I think," she says, nodding. "Thank you."

I have to hand it to her, she seems like a compassionate person. In the same situation she finds herself in, not that many people would have their friend on their mind before anything else. I wish I could do something to give her some peace of mind about this Moxie girl, but honestly, I'm more surprised than anything that she *isn't* a groupie. She sounds like the type.

Kate, though, is more of a puzzle, and I wonder what she's going to be like as soon as we do have a chance to stop running.

She could bolt and find the nearest cop to talk to. She could bolt in the *wrong* direction and wind up in the club's hands all over again. I don't want to think what they'd do to her now that she's tied to Roadster's death. Sure, she didn't kill him, and one look at the body would make it clear that it was my brass knuckles that did the deed. Still, there's no telling whether Buzz will be anything approaching reasonable if he gets his hands on either of us.

I'd sooner cut those fat fingers off myself than let Buzz lay a single one of them on Kate. I don't know why I feel protective of her. Hell, I've just killed for her, a perfect stranger. I did that because I can't be party to sex trafficking like that, but now, I feel like it's personal. I can't explain it, but I feel it, and right now, feelings are all I've got.

Why did Buzz choose her of all the women in Wyoming?

I can't spare it thought right now. Even though the feel of the bike between my thighs puts me at ease, we're still in danger, and I need to put every ounce of energy into keeping us out of the MC's way.

"Are those guys... were they your friends?" she asks, probably desperate for what feels like some human contact in the middle of a terrifying situation.

"Thought so," I reply curtly.

"What was going to happen to me?" she asks.

I say nothing in reply. I can't. It would be no use to terrify her with what Buzz had in mind, and she already has more than enough reason to agree that running from the club is the only option right now. Besides, there's that other niggling issue of whether she'll put pressure from the authorities on me once we're clear of the gang.

Anything that could lead back to me is a threat. Hell, this whole insane rescue plan I pulled out of my ass is probably going to get me killed. But if that's the way it's got to be, I'd rather go down fighting for what I believe in than selling my soul. That doesn't mean I can't play it smart, though. I can't trust her yet, not completely.

Maybe not even a little.

I check my mirror every few minutes, and eventually, I lose the sight of headlights far behind me. I'm weighted down a little with Kate on the back, but the club is traveling as a group and taking time to search stops and towns for signs of us. That's slowing them down just enough. Then again, Big Daddy's bike was at that motel alone, so they could be splitting up in towns to save time. Damn them, this is the same thing I'd be doing if I were hunting a guy like me.

I need a new plan. The longer we're on the road like this, the more this will just become a game of who can endure the longest. And the simple fact is that the club will probably be able to outlast us if it comes to that.

Gas will, eventually, become an issue.

I don't have long to mull that over.

On a long stretch of highway with very little visible ahead or behind us, the clouds cover the moon and cast us into darker shadows than ever before. I let the chill settle in and brace myself to push on to the next town, hopefully one that the club hasn't gotten to yet.

But my plans like to blow up in my face tonight, it seems.

BANG!

I didn't see whatever it was—it might have been a nail, or a piece of shrapnel from an accident on the road earlier today, or even just something washed onto the asphalt after the rains. Whatever it is, it's just sharp enough to pierce my tire, and Kate screams as we start spinning out.

"Fuck, fuck, fuck!" I curse as we spin, and I do everything I can to steer the bike to the side of the road as it comes to a grinding halt.

We're stranded with no transportation, and my bike has just breathed its last.

Silence.

It's all just silence.

And then, from the darkness comes a deafening thump-thump-thump. I'm so disoriented and dizzy with fear that it takes me a good few seconds to recognize the sound as my own heartbeat. My blood is rushing loudly in my ears, as though every inch of my body is thrumming with powerful terror. I feel sick to my stomach, and as fearful as I was on the back of this motorcycle when it was moving, it's nothing whatsoever compared to the raw, unfettered horror of sitting on the back of it when it's dead still.

It all happened so quickly. First, we were riding along at top speed, and my faith in Breaker was just high enough for me to believe maybe, just maybe we could outpace the rest of the gang behind us.

But now?

I have no idea what's going to happen to us. Dread seeps in at the edges of my mind, poisoning my thoughts and making me feel numb all over. There's nothing I can do. Nothing I can offer in this silent moment. I just know they're going to catch us. They're going to show up any second now with their baring bike engines and their scowls and their evil, evil intentions. I can so vividly in my mind's eye the drama unfolding: the guys picking me off the back of this bike and dragging me away from Breaker. The gang circling in around him like a pride of lions closing in on the weakest wildebeest on the savanna. Moving in for the kill.

I wonder: will they kill me, too? Or is there an even darker fate than death on the horizon for me now? I swallow hard, feeling as though I might be sick. It's too quiet without the rumbling engine to keep my horrid fears at bay.

"What happened?" I manage to choke out between stunned breaths.

"Popped a tire. Warped the metal. It's over with," Breaker growls.

"It's… over?" I repeat, stricken with terror. If he's given up, that's it. He was my only hope. Without him, I'm completely helpless out here. Will he hand me over willingly? Will he use me as a bargaining chip? My life in exchange for mercy on his own?

But before I can fully embrace that dark future, Breaker snakes an arm around my waist and hoists me off of the bike in one swift, easy movement. I yelp with fear as my heels hit the muddy ground. The motorcycle, dead and ruined, collapses on its side with a sickening crunch. I stare at it open-mouthed and wide-eyed, feeling every last thread of hope unravel around me.

"Wh-what do we do now? Oh god. We're going to die," I whimper, feeling the harsh sting of hot tears prickling in my eyes. "We're going to die."

"Like hell we are," Breaker snarls.

He grabs my hand and yanks me away from the broken bike. I stumble as he drags me along behind him, his much longer and thicker legs pumping rapidly as he breaks into a full-on sprint. I gasp for breath, my heart pounding and my own legs quaking with fear. Exhaustion overwhelms me and the blood rushes out of my head, my vision swimming as I get too dizzy to see straight. The world around me tilts in a sick angle, like I've been tilted sideways.

I try to will my legs to carry me faster, to keep up with Breaker's dashing pace. But I've simply gone on too long without food, water, or rest. The full-body fatigue hits me like a freight train to the face and even though I cling desperately to his hand with my own clammy fingers, I can't stop myself from crumpling to the damp earth, the world tilting on its axis. For a moment, Breaker still tries to pull me along, despite the fact that my knees are dragging the ground.

"I-I'm sorry. I'm so tired," I whimper weakly. "I can't… I can't keep up."

My chest heaves with exertion, my head tingling with dizziness. I try to summon the strength to get upright again, but it's just too much. All the pain, all the fear, all the hours without sustenance or rest have caught up to me at the absolute worst possible time. It occurs to me, even through the fog in my head, that this could spell the end for me. This could be the night I die. Breaker is under no obligation to wait for me. He can move at a pace far beyond what I could offer even under the best circumstances, and these are the worst circumstances imaginable.

But to my surprise, Breaker doesn't desert me. Instead, he skids to a stop, swivels around on his heels, and scoops me up into his arms as though I weigh nothing at all. All I can do is drape limply against his chest as he breaks into a full run again, cradling me in his arms like some kind of life-size ragdoll. It's nearly pitch-black by now, the moon blocked out by a gathering of dark purplish clouds. In the distance, I can still hear the ominous, echoing rumble of motorcycle engines as they thunder along toward us. We have nothing at our disposal but our bodies and the clothes on our backs. No weapons. No safeguards. Nothing at all.

And yet, Breaker has not given up on me. There's no way on earth he can see exactly where he's going, and still he bolts through the night like a bat out of hell, keeping me safe in his muscular arms. Against my cheek, I can feel his heart beating. Ba-bump. Ba-bump. To my surprise and amazement, it's not even an accelerated heartbeat. Even under this extreme duress, he seems even-keeled and in control.

No matter what fate befalls us at the end of this dash, I have to admire his tenacity and self-control. He doesn't let the fear grip him the way it clutches me in a vice. He just takes stock of the situation and reacts accordingly. It's awe-inspiring to watch, especially from here. Once my vision stops blurring so badly, I look up at him. I see the sharp, heavy cut of his jaw, his mouth set in a hard line as he carries me along. His muscles clench and tense as he holds me close, clasping me to his chest with all the strength and fierceness of a beast defending its territory. He's overwhelmingly strong, and I can't help but feel so protected in his arms. The moon slowly slides out from behind the clouds, and from my vantage point below, it almost looks as though the unearthly pale glow forms a sort of makeshift halo around Breaker's head. My savior. My angel.

My protector.

I have no reason to trust him, and yet what choice do I have?

Especially since I can still hear bikes rumbling in the distance, reminding me that trouble and danger are lurking close behind, nipping at our heels.

"I can still hear them," I murmur faintly. "They're coming for us, Breaker."

"I know," he replies softly without missing a beat. "But don't worry. Sound travels fast through the valley. They aren't as close as they seem to be. We still have time, Kate. You just hold on tight."

I want to believe him. I want to pretend that everything will be okay and that we'll escape this chase unscathed. That we will both live to see the crowning light of morning and breathe a gasp of free air once again. But my hope is dwindling along with my strength. My body is so fragile now. I feel as though I must be made of dust, easily scattered by one strong gust of wind.

"How can you say that? How can you know?" I ask him in a soft, timid voice. I don't want to argue with him, but my pessimism is showing through. I can't see a way out of this.

"Kate," he says gently, and I know it's warning, but I can't stop. I'm too scared.

"They're going to find your bike and they'll know where we went," I ramble on weakly. "They're going to figure it all out, Breaker, and then they'll find us."

"You're right," he agrees. I'm taken aback by his ready answer, and my stomach lurches with anxiety. But then he goes on. "They will find my bike. They will keep looking. But you have to trust me, okay? You have to trust that I will do everything in my power to keep you safe from them, Kate."

I want so badly to trust his pledge. But all I feel is emptiness. All I can think of is defeat. Over and over again, those dark images flood my thoughts. The bikers catching up to us. Surrounding us. Tearing me out of Breaker's strong, protective grasp. Wrenching us apart. Ripping him to pieces and taking me away to torture and sell. I know this fate is looming, hovering just over us like a dark miasma. I can't fully believe in Breaker's words, but I do know that I have to trust him. What choice do I have otherwise?

He keeps running, his legs carrying us farther and farther away from the main road where his motorbike lies destroyed. He jostles me every now and then in his arms, almost as though he wants to make sure I stay awake. I don't totally understand why, but I assume it has something to do with dead weight. Or maybe he just knows that I'm mere inches away from totally passing out, and he needs me alert and vigilant if we're going to make it out of this situation alive. We keep going despite my fear, despite how tired I know he must be by now. But if he's getting fatigued, he sure as hell isn't showing it.

In fact, he's barely breathing any harder than he was before. He must be very strong to keep me cradled in his arms like this for so long without having to take a break. I know I may not be the heaviest load to heft around, but I'm still a full-grown young woman. I'm not weightless, though I may as well be in Breaker's arms. He doesn't give up, not even when the darkness settles in like a velvety curtain around us, clouds blotting out the moon and stars once again. He runs and runs, never stopping to even catch a breath, until finally I tilt my head and happen to clock a looming shadow growing taller and broader in front of us. That must be our destination. A shack in the middle of nowhere.

As we approach the shack, Breaker comes to a halt and gently sets me down on my feet. I wobble a little at first, the dizziness swarming my brain. Then the world stops spinning and I stand on my own two feet, even though my heart is racing.

"What's happening? Why are we here?" I ask, looking around for any sign of life.

"I'm here to grab something," Breaker answers. "Can I trust you to stay put?"

"Here? Alone?" I murmur, eyes wide.

He nods and puts both hands on my shoulders. "Yes. Not for long, Kate, but yes. Can I count on you to stand here and wait for me?" he asks.

Tears well up in my eyes. "I-I guess so. Why can't I come with you?" I whisper.

"I'll be quicker on my own. It's important, okay? Just stay here," he insists.

"Okay," I reply, nodding. "Okay."

"Good girl. I'll be back as soon as I can," Breaker says, and with that, he dashes off into the shadowy darkness.

I watch him disappear into the night, feeling

sicker and weaker by the second. I want to trust him. I want to believe he's going to come back for me as he claims, but still there's a part of me demanding to make a run for it. The urge is almost overwhelming. But I clamp it down and force myself to stay put and do as I'm told.

Not long after, I hear an engine splutter to life, and to my surprise, a beat-up but functional black sedan comes rolling toward me from behind the shack. I stumble back, clapping a hand over my heart, until I manage to make out Breaker's face through the windshield. He pulls up beside me and pushes the passenger door open.

"Come on," he says hastily. "Get in."

He doesn't have to tell me twice.

I climb into the seat and yank the door shut, then turn to him and ask confusedly, "Where did you get this car? Whose is it?"

"Belongs to a friend of mine. He runs a garage right off the highway. It's a great business model because people break down out here all the time," he explains vaguely.

"Does your friend know you stole his car?" I press him.

"It's better you not know," he answers.

"Oh," I mumble softly. Fair enough.

"Kate, I need you to do something for me," Breaker says, glancing over at me intently.

"What is it?" I ask.

"I need you to tell me everything you saw and heard of the men who put you in that room. Give me as much detail as you can," he says. "It's important."

I bite my lip, toying for a moment with the idea of lying. But then he shoots me a look that makes me change my mind. I'd better be honest. At least with him.

"I was at a club with my friend Moxie. Some guy brought us there in a taxi. She was drinking with him at the bar. I stayed around to keep an eye on her, but when I went to the bathroom, they both disappeared. Then a man came up to me and said he would help me find her. From there it gets a little hazy," I sigh, pinching the bridge of my nose. "I was in a vehicle of some kind. The backseat or the trunk, I think. I remember the tires crunching over dirt and gravel. And then I woke up in that awful room. I was alone. I was still wearing my clothes from the night before so I assumed… I assumed everything was fine. Until I realized the door was locked from the outside. And the window was bolted shut. Then I got scared."

"Go on," he urges me, even though I can see the rage on his face.

"There's not much else I remember. I'm sorry," I murmur, shaking my head. "I banged on the door. I felt so sick. Someone must have drugged me. I promise I wasn't drunk. I'm only eighteen. I can't even order alcohol. I was just drinking plain cranberry juice, but I was so fuzzy and confused."

"Mhm," he says, looking even more pissed off than before.

"I'm sorry. Am I making you mad?" I ask in a tiny voice.

He looks over at me, and the pain etched in his gaze makes my heart pang.

"No. I'm not mad at you, Kate. But I am angry," he says cryptically.

I'm having a hard time reading him in the dim light of the console, but when I glance out the window, I feel a shock of familiarity. I see a sign—which clearly states that we're headed toward Stonedale. I sit up straighter in the seat, excited.

"That's my hometown!" I gasp, pointing at the sign as we pass.

"I know," he says grimly. "But don't get your hopes up. The Prez is coming for you, Kate, and he doesn't let anybody go easy."

BREAKER

The blackness on the horizon starts to melt away into a visible blue, and I know sunrise is right around the corner. There's something so overwhelmingly comforting about what seems like a subtle shift in color. But on a primal, basic level, it tells me that the day is about to begin, and I'm eager to take any comfort I can get out here on the road.

The sedan has been holding up nicely. It isn't the most comfortable ride on the planet, but it's a hell of a lot better than having to deal with Buzz and the rest of the club hot on our tails. I haven't seen hide nor hair of them since we shook them off last, which is a relief, I have to admit. My best guess is that they saw my bike on the side of the road and started spending more time searching off-road. I could be anywhere out there in the desert, and the one thing they almost definitely aren't expecting is for us to have gotten another ride so quickly.

Kate is sitting in the passenger's seat, but she seems to have barely blinked, much less gotten any sleep. I've been expecting her to nod off at any moment, but she's on high alert still. When that energy runs out, it's going to run out hard and fast. I haven't slept either, and I'm used to doing all-nighters like this. She isn't exactly a spoiled princess, but I have a feeling she hasn't spent many nights on the run without food or rest.

Letting your body be in fight-or-flight mode for that long takes a toll on you. It won't be long before the cracks start to show on her. I need to be ready when that happens, because today is going to make or break this rescue.

The darkest blue in the distance starts to creep upward, pushed away by the warm orange glow of the sunrise proper. Finally, I see the sliver of that burning orange orb on the east side of the north-ward-bound road, and it begins its ascent.

When I glance over at it, I can't help but notice that the light seems to frame Kate's face as she stares forward vacantly. She looks exhausted, but even so, her natural beauty gives her a kind of quiet dignity that keeps her head held high.

I tear my eyes away just half a second before she

glances over at me, sensing my gaze. I can't keep looking over at her like this. Maybe I should double-check myself and make sure I'm not the one whose judgment is starting to go haywire. This is a scared girl I'm rescuing, nothing more than that. Of course she's beautiful, Buzz wouldn't have kidnapped her if she wasn't.

But that thought makes me feel bad the moment it crosses my mind, so I dismiss it. I don't know what to think of the girl next to me, except that she needs me, whether she likes it or not.

Once dawn is well underway, we're able to see the town of Stonedale up ahead. It shouldn't be that much longer before we reach it now, and I'm sure that's doing wonders to keep Kate awake, but it's a lot more exciting for her than it is for me.

I could just drop her off and disappear. I know of a gas station just far enough outside Stonedale that I could stop there, let her go to the bathroom, and be completely out of sight by the time she gets out. She could use a pay phone, get a ride home, and… be promptly taken by the club again the second they catch up to her. And they *will* catch up to her.

Buzz is not a kind man. I've been able to turn a blind eye to some of the way he acts over the years, but not this. I can excuse him beating a rival too hard. I can't excuse selling people's bodies for money like he was planning on doing. Even if I was welcomed back with open arms, I wouldn't consider any offer Buzz would put on the table. I know men like him all too well.

If he's willing to hurt a woman like that, it just means he's willing to throw anyone he sees as lesser than him under the bus without a second thought. As long as he thinks he can get away with it, a man like that will not hesitate. I've had too many step-fathers walk out on my mom or do even worse to her for less. It's a fact of men like that I've come to learn over the years, and I can't just abandon Kate to that fate.

"Hey," I say, and she jumps, sucking in a quick gasp of air at my sudden speech.

"Sorry," she says, shaking her head and rubbing her temples. "I've just been zoning out watching Stonedale get closer."

"About that," I say, taking a deep breath and rolling my shoulders back to stretch my muscles out. Her eyes follow the movements of my body, and I force myself to ignore that.

"We're still going there, right?" she asks with a hint of worry in her voice.

"Yeah. But I need to make something crystal-goddamn-clear before we get there," I say, holding a finger out and looking sternly at her, which seems to make her recoil, and she nods softly. "The second I drop you off—and I mean *the second*—you need to leave Stonedale. Permanently."

Her jaw drops, and I watch the color drain from her already weary face. She looks like she might be faint for a second, but she snaps out of it and shakes her head vigorously.

"You've got to be kidding me!" she blurts. "There's… there's no way I can do that, Breaker. I can't leave Stonedale, it's all I've got! I don't have anywhere else to go, I-I… my job is in Stonedale, all my friends, I-"

"Doesn't matter," I growl, and she twitches uneasily. "Pick a place. Haven't you ever just stared at a map and thought about different places you'd run off to if you had the chance? Throw everything into a suitcase, pick a direction, and drive until you can't drive anymore? I sure hope so, sweetheart, because with Buzz and the rest of the club on your tail, that's exactly what you're going to have to do. I'm deadly serious, and you better pay attention."

My tone is harsh and stern, and she reacts accordingly. Her eyes have been looking at me with growing interest over the drive, but now, I have to hold back my sadness as I watch all that evaporate and get replaced with fear. She's a prisoner all over again, and she swallows, trying to keep her composure.

"It's not that easy, Breaker," she says. I notice she's using my name a lot, trying to keep me sympathetic to her by making me feel like we're on the same side. I wish I could tell her that's not necessary. I wish I could clear the air, but I'm going to have to scare this stubborn-ass girl if she won't do as she's told for her own good.

"Isn't it?" I snap. "I've done it plenty of times since I was younger than you."

Her jaw tenses, and she tries to dig her heels in. This is going to be harder than I thought, but I have to admire the tenacity of the girl.

"I'm eighteen, asshole!" she says with a trembling voice. "I don't exactly have a savings account I can fall back on!"

"Then you had better find a relative or a friend who owes you a favor *real* goddamn fast, Kate," I snarl, shooting a piercing gaze over at her, "because I don't think you get what we're up against here. I've watched Buzz put a bullet in a man he called a friend for running a side-hustle without telling him, and every single one of those guys under him is capable of just as much, including me," I add.

"Breaker," she breathes through a clenched jaw, eyes looking more heart-wrenching by the moment, but I can't back down.

"If you're anywhere near this town, they're going to find you," I say with terrifying finality. "And when they do, don't you think for a second they'll hesitate from dragging out of your cozy little bed kicking and screaming."

"I'll call the police!" she says fiercely.

"And tell them what, Kate?" I demand. "That 'some gruff looking bikers' kidnapped you, but a nice one brought you home after a night drinking? You think a bunch of small-town cops are going to give a shit about that?"

My harsh words give her some pause, and I press on. I'm going for the throat, and I can feel my heart ripping into pieces to say it, but I need to put the fear of the devil into her, because that's what's after us.

"You really want to know what Buzz had in mind for you, little girl?" I say, nostrils flaring as I glare between her and the road. "He bought a fucking dive bar outside Rawlins, and he was going to turn it into a strip club—and not the legit kind, either. He was going to pimp you out to every crusty old fucker who came through with enough cash in hand to make Buzz happy and force you to warm their beds for the night. And that's assuming Buzz wouldn't just take you for himself."

Her face looks aghast, but she's barely reacting anymore. She looks like she's seen a ghost, and I know that my words are finally hitting home where I need them to. But I can't decide what's worse: the fact that I have to twist the knife like this, or the fact that every single word out of my mouth is true. I might be scaring her, but I'm not going to lie to her.

I've run with bad men in the past. I don't know

what that makes me, but all that matters is what I do now.

"And if you think they need to stick to Wyoming to do that, you're kidding yourself," I go on. "If I were Buzz, I'd be tracking you down, packing you up, and heading to greener pastures as soon as I could sell that shitty bar. But that guy I killed back there was his son. If they get their hands on me, they're going to rip me apart piece by piece, probably leave my body burning in a pile of trash somewhere I won't be found for a few years. And if he gets his hands on you when he's in a bad mood, he might just have a mind to do the same thing and cut his losses. You're money to him, Kate, and nothing more."

A new sound makes me turn my attention back to Kate, and my heart plummets as I realize there are tears streaming down her red-rimmed eyes. Her lip is quivering, and her whole face is going blotchy red.

"Ah, shit," I grumble before she turns her head and tries to wipe her eyes dry, but as soon as she feels how wet they are, she starts sobbing. I open and close my mouth a few times, fighting the urge to say something comforting, but I know damn well I can't.

Can't blame her either, really.

The sun is up now, and the heat is starting to set in. With nobody on the road ahead of us or behind us, I slowly pull over and come to a stop.

"Wh- what are you doing?" she asks through

sobs, sniffing and looking up at me in terror. She looks so vulnerable and fragile that my heart aches for her. I can't just let her sob all the way to Stonedale. Besides, pulling up at a gas station with a terrified, tired, crying girl is a good way to get my ass caught by the cops.

"Giving you a minute," I say calmly as I put on the emergency brake. "I'm taking the keys, so don't try anything funny."

Before she can reply, I open the door and feel the dry air flood the car. I walk around the car and take a deep breath, trudging off the road while Kate's bloodshot eyes follow me ruefully. I take my phone out and turn it on for the first time in a while, deciding to do what I've been avoiding and actually look at who's been trying to get in touch with me.

I'm about ten yards from the car when I finally feel the buzzes of messages and voicemails hitting my phone. Scrolling through the notifications, my frown deepens, because there are sadly no surprises.

"Breaker. I don't know if you're reading this, but bring the girl back. Let's talk this out." Bones's message doesn't exactly radiate subtlety.

"Prez is looking for you, Breaker. This is not a game." Ironside sounds almost like a warning, unless my eyes are fooling me. I have to wonder if there's more to the guy than meets the eye after all, but I'm in no position to make that call right now.

"If you're a real man, get your ass back here,

with the girl, and face me." Buzz's text tells me everything I need to know. He's not interested in patching things up, and if I go back to them, I'm faced with death.

There are also a number of calls and voicemails on the phone from other contacts, even a few numbers I don't recognize. I don't bother with them. I know all I need to know: the club wants me to come back with Kate, and it sounds like my only reward for cooperating from here on out might be a quick death. And I'm not so sure about that last part.

I know I have to destroy this phone. The guys aren't exactly the most tech savvy on the planet, but I don't want to risk them tracking me if they have half the opportunity to. I exit all the messages, leaving nothing but my phone background wallpaper on the screen.

It's a picture of me and my mom at the most recent birthday of hers I was able to go to. The sight of it gives me pause. Up until now, I've been thinking hard about the fact that I'm forcing Kate to uproot and leave her hometown, but it hasn't fully settled in yet that I'm going to have to go into hiding too. Buzz is probably going to be after me harder than Kate, even.

I don't know how much more I'll be able to get in touch with Mom safely.

"What are you looking at?"

Kate's voice behind me snaps me out of my trance, and I clench my jaw, shutting off the phone screen and dropping it to the ground. A second after it hits the dust, I bring the heel of my boot down on the back of it, smashing it to pieces with a few quick stomps that make Kate gasp and step back.

"Making sure they don't track us, that's all," I grunt.

"Was that your phone?" she asks.

"Yeah. It's done now. Feeling any better?" I say, turning to face her and step forward.

"I…" she hesitates, still looking on the verge of tears. "No."

"Me neither," I admit in a softer tone, glancing back at my phone. We stand there staring at each other for a few moments, and it hits me just how tired both of us are, from the way we look to the way we feel and speak. The wind howls in the distance, and I realize that my glare isn't nearly as harsh as it was a few minutes ago. I don't think I have it in me anymore.

"I know I can't go back home," she says at last, swallowing hard. "I… I'm sorry I overreacted."

I wince and step forward, then start to open my arms to her. I do it slowly enough to back out carly if she looks too intimidated, but to my surprise and relief, she takes the invitation readily and nearly melts into the gruff hug I wrap around her. Her body trembles for a moment, and I feel a tear stain the front of my shirt.

"I know I can't go back," she breathes again, repeating it more to herself than anything. "This is just… a lot."

"I know," I say.

"And I can't abandon Moxie," she says, stepping back and looking up at me firmly. "I'll never go near a biker bar as long as I live, I swear, a-and I'll scrounge up whatever I've got in my account and use my credit cards to get me out of this county. I don't know where yet, but I-I can make it happen. I just can't do it before finding my friend. Please, Breaker, will you help me?"

There's such desperate, vulnerable hope in her voice that I know damn well I can't say no. I run my hand over my face, then look long and hard at her, jaw tight. She'll be more trouble than she's worth if I can't get her to chill out about her friend.

"I need you to swear to me," I say, holding out that finger again, "that if I help you find Moxie, you get your ass out of town, away from here, anywhere you can go, A-S-A-P," I spell out. "Cut all ties, leave all phones, drop off social media, maybe even change your name, just stay away as long as you live. If you want to live, and you want me to help you get back with Moxie, that's what you're going to do, got it? And forget about so much as looking at any biker from now on."

She listens to every word I say with rapt attention, her face scared but determined, and that makes
the next words out of her mouth without missing a
beat all the more surprising:

"What about you?"

I immediately feel my cheeks start to flush a bright, sheepish pink when the question rolls off my tongue. What the hell is wrong with my brain that I would've thought for even half a second it was an okay statement to make? I stare at Breaker with my eyes widening as the meaning of my question sinks in. I bite my lip, feeling like a complete cool for asking that.

Why would I ever actually want to see this guy again? After everything we have been through, after how much he has frightened me, after I watched him so easily kill his fellow club member right in front of me, what madness would have to take over my mind to make think it would be at all good to run into him again? Once is quite enough for this lifetime, I try to remind myself inwardly. But I can't pretend like my question isn't based in a real, genuine sense of bonding I feel with my captor-turned-savior. I can sort of remember learning about the Stockholm Syndrome phenomenon back in high school civics. Perhaps that is the culprit behind my burgeoning feelings of warmth and admiration for Breaker. By all rights, I should be afraid of him. Terrified, actually. That would be the smart way to react to a guy like him in my life. But whenever I try to think of him in that negative light, my memory instantly flashes back to the feeling of being cradled so delicately, so protectively in his powerful arms as he bolted away from the scene of his motorbike breakdown. The way he so softly said my name, like it was something precious, like it was a secret word in a secret language only the two of us could comprehend. Like the one simple syllable of my name tasted so sweet upon his tongue that he could only grant it the reverence it deserves.

Nobody has ever said my name quite like that before. Never before have I felt this wild, restless, longing energy pulsate through my body every time Breaker stands close to me. He makes my heart beat faster. He makes every nerve in my body burst into lightning bolts, firing on all cylinders. There's an aura of heat and strength radiating from him that I find both terrifying and intoxicating at the same time.

He is a representation of the horrific time I spent in captivity, of the bent trajectory of my life that will lead me away from my family, away from my friends, away from my prescribed future and everything I once knew so well. I should hate him. I most definitely should fear him, and I do. But there's something else crackling intensely between us, and it isn't just because he's stunningly, ruggedly hot as hell. It's more than that, even if I can't quite put my finger on it. I crave him. I ache for him to stay close by. My body pulses with the desire to fold myself up into his strong arms again, the only safe space I have encountered in the past forty-eight hours.

Still, I know I shouldn't want to see him again. He may have saved me from one hellishly dark fate, but he's still a dangerous man in his own right. I should fear him, not desire him. It almost feels like the wires have gotten crossed in my mind in regards to Breaker. I want what I should fear. Then again, I *am* incredibly sleep-deprived, exhausted, starving, thirsty, and traumatized by the events of the past day or two. It makes sense that my objective reasoning abilities are, uh, a little slowed down at the moment. Hopefully they'll kick back in soon, though, because I know now that my journey is only just beginning.

To both my relief and my dismay, Breaker doesn't answer my pointed question. Instead, he just fixes me with yet another version of an unreadable scowl. He gestures toward the stolen black sedan and sighs.

"Come on, kid. It's time to go," he says quietly. "Back in the car."

I slowly turn and watch as he strides around to the driver's side, opens the door, and slides behind the steering wheel. I stand there for a moment, paralyzed with indecision. I know I should probably just do as he says. After all, he knows far better than I do what's at stake here. But I also know that if I take this step, any step, it will only bring me closer to the worst thing I will ever have to do: desert my hometown life and strike out into the world on my own.

"I don't know if I'm ready," I murmur sadly.

Breaker looks confused at first, thinking I'm referring just to getting in the car. But then the real meaning behind my words dawns on him and his intense face softens a little.

"I know, Kate. It's difficult. But you need to do as I say if you want any shot at surviving this mess," he insists. I sigh, knowing he's right.

I reluctantly climb back into the passenger's seat and close the door, slumping back against the seat and leaning to rest my forehead against the fogged-up window. I give a little yelp and startle at the sensation of Breaker's large, warm hand touching my knee. I whip around to look at him, and the fire blazing behind his eyes is almost too much to see.

"I need you to help me retrace your steps," he says. "Can you do that for me?"

I bite my lip and nod slowly. "I-I can try."

"Good girl. Now, where is this club your friend took you to?" he asks.

"I'm not totally sure. It's in a rough part of town, a neighborhood I don't usually go to," I admitted. "It was a biker bar, I think. There were strippers and scary men. Motorcycles parked out back. Big neon sign with some of the letters burned out."

"Can you remember what the sign said?" he presses me.

I hang my head sadly. "No. I'm sorry. I think I was too distracted trying to look after Moxie. I didn't read the sign," I say.

It hits me all of a sudden just how much time has passed since I first went out that fateful evening with my friend. It's been over thirty-six hours at least since I last saw Moxie. We have to find her. I'm terrified that she might have fallen into the same trap that I found myself in. After all, she's a pretty young thing, too. And she's much more personable and outgoing than me. I'm sure she looks like an easy target to the kind of guy who would seek out young women to capture for… dark purposes.

"I can figure it out from that. It's a small town," Breaker assures me.

"I wish you hadn't destroyed your cell phone," I speak up suddenly. "I could have used it to call Moxie's cell and see where she is."

Breaker arches a thick, dark eyebrow and glances

over at me with an expression akin to amusement on his handsome face.

"What? What is it?" I ask, feeling self-conscious.

"Nothing. It's just surprising that you would have her phone number memorized. I thought most kids these days didn't bother learning any numbers by heart," he points out.

It's my turn now to look bemused. "I'm eighteen, Breaker. I'm not a small child. We're closer in age than you think. Your generation can't be that much different from mine," I remark, surprised at my own boldness.

"That's a fair point," Breaker agrees. "I suppose we're more alike than dissimilar. But there's still a damn good reason why I would not have let you use my cell phone even if I hadn't crushed it with my boot."

"Why? I don't understand. You want to find this club so we can find Moxie, but it would be so much easier to find her with a phone. Trust me, she doesn't go anywhere without it," I say.

"Because the motorcycle club will be tracking it, that's why. The last thing we need right now is to place a phone call that will ping off all those towers and give those guys a triangulated location so they can swarm us and take you back from me," Breaker explains. "Beyond that, it would put your friend in danger, too. The best we can hope for is that she has somehow evaded capture or involvement so far. But if her phone received a call from my phone, that would put her on the map. She would be in even more trouble."

"Oh. That makes sense," I begrudgingly accept.

We ride along in near-silence for a few minutes before my own curiosity comes springing out of my mouth, uncontrolled and unfettered. "Breaker, I don't understand how you ended up getting involved in all this mess in the first place. Why are you with those biker guys? You seem so… so good. Why would you fall in with bad guys like them?" I blurted out.

"There's not so big a difference between them and me," he says somberly. "We have more in common than you think."

"I don't believe that for a second," I insist. "None of those other guys would help me."

"That doesn't mean I'm better than they are. It just means you got lucky," he grunts.

But that's not good enough for me. "No. I don't buy it. Breaker, you saved my life. You risked your own life to save me. That makes you a good man. Those other guys back there… they're not good men. I can tell. I just don't get how you would end up tangled up with these losers. You're better than that," I tell him defiantly.

"I don't want to discuss this shit with you," he warns.

But I can't help it. He's acting so shifty and

uncomfortable, which only stokes my curiosity. I want a fuller picture. I want the details. I want to understand. I decide to try a different tactic to get Breaker to open up to me, though I know it has a chance of backfiring and just pissing him off even more. At the moment, I hardly care. I'm already screwed. I might as well ask my silly questions while I'm still alive for the time being.

"I saw the woman on your phone screen before you smashed it," I murmur softly. "She's really pretty. Is she your girlfriend or something?"

Breaker's jaw tenses and he shakes his head slowly. "No. She's not."

"Your sister?" I press him doggedly. "Your mother?"

"Bingo. But it doesn't matter," he says flatly.

"It's really sweet that you had a picture of her as your background. That must mean you really care about her, huh?" I suggest.

Breaker's hands grip the steering wheel more tightly, his knuckles going white. I can tell I'm tapdancing right on an exposed nerve, but I can't back down. I want more information about the man who saved me. I want to find out as much detail as humanly possible, even though he seems totally reluctant to give any of it up to me.

"It's not," he retorts.

"What do you mean? I think it's cute," I say with a shrug.

"It isn't. I have not spoken to my mother in many years. I wish you hadn't seen that damn photo of her," he growls. I can tell I might have pushed him too far. He even sounds a little ashamed that I saw it, though I don't have any idea why.

"I have a weird relationship with my parents, too," I pipe up, wanting to smooth things over as I always do. "They're hardly ever around because they work so much. And I have four siblings, so their attention is always split in five different directions on the rare occasion when they *are* home. But they're still overprotective. They want me to stay home all the time, never go out, never try new things. Sometimes at my house I feel like some kind of caged bird. I want to be free, but I also want them to want me around, if that makes sense."

For a moment I worry I might have overshared, but then Breaker nods.

"I get that," he replies. "Must have made it even worse for you when the guys locked you up in that room."

"It's totally not the same," I insist quickly, then when I think about it some more, I add, "Well, maybe a little bit the same."

Again, a few more minutes of quiet. I can tell Breaker isn't usually the kind of guy to give away anything easily. He keeps his thoughts to himself. I can't help but wonder why. Is it just the way he is? Is it because he's gone so long without anyone around to ask him? Does nobody in his life care about these answers but me?

There's something else weighing heavily on my mind. I have to set it free, come what may. It might make him angry, but I have to know.

"Breaker," I begin softly, "what happened back there?"

"Back where?" he asks, clearly trying to avoid the subject. But I'm stubborn.

"Back at the place where they had me locked up. I heard a scuffle. You opened the door. I saw a body on the floor. There was a lot of blood around his head, Breaker," I mention.

He frowns deeply. "Don't ask me about that," he commands.

"I'm sorry. I know it's a… a sore spot. But I need to ask it. I need to know if I'm riding in the car right now with a killer," I tell him emphatically.

"Would it make any difference?" he points out, glaring at me.

I shake my head. "No. I just want to know the answer."

He groans and rakes his fingers back through his thick hair. "I wasn't sure if he was dead when we left the scene, but judging by the messages I've been receiving from the rest of the club, I'm pretty certain now that he did die," Breaker explains to me with an almost clinical detachment. I expected to feel sick to

my stomach, but instead I just feel kind of…
relieved.

Oh god, what is wrong with me?

"How do you feel about that?" I ask with genuine interest.

"What are you, a shrink?" he snaps.

I remain patient and quiet. "It's just a question, Breaker. I'm not psychoanalyzing you or anything. I promise," I tell him.

"You want to know how I feel?" he growls. "I feel angry. I feel pissed the hell off that Roadster put me in that situation to begin with. I trusted him. I thought of him as my friend. It never should have happened, but he's the one who pushed me to that point."

"I'm sorry about your friend," I murmur.

He bristles at the apology. I can tell Breaker is a man who does not like to accept pity or compassion from others, especially not a girl like me.

"And if you tell any living soul about what I did to Roadster, I will have to find you and take care of you myself," he adds threateningly.

The old sedan creaks as I turn it off the road and into the cracking parking lot of the club that Kate has pointed out to me, and I drive it around to the side of the building before parking and turning the ignition off. I look at Kate thoughtfully for a moment, and she furrows her brow, shifting uncomfortably.

"What?" she asks.

"Trying to decide whether to bring you in with me or leave you out here," I say.

"What, do you think I'll run?" she asks, frowning. "I need you to help me find Moxie, remember? Why would I run?"

This puts me in an interesting position, for a reason I wasn't expecting. On the one hand, what she's saying isn't entirely accurate. If she really wanted to make a run for it right now, she could still find a cop, say the right things, and get some help finding Moxie without me. I haven't gotten to know everything about Kate as a person, but I can tell she's clever and persistent. She's the kind of person who I reckon could make anything happen if she put her mind to it, and I wonder how aware of that she is.

But that's not what's giving me pause. It's the fact that I don't think she's lying. I'm no psychic, but I can pick out people's tells for lying pretty easily, and I don't sense any dishonesty in Kate. I think that if I leave her here, she really won't run off.

"Fine," she says, "I need to use the bathroom anyway, so I'll come in with you if it'll make you feel better."

I chuckle. "Well, if you're volunteering."

We climb out and approach the club, and it looks vaguely familiar to me. It's more or less one big box-shaped building that could be mistaken for a warehouse, and it might have even been that at some point long ago. Now, it sports a single door front entrance that's covered in posters and stickers of various kinds, but there's another doorway around the back.

The place looks locked up still, and I figure it probably won't open for another few hours, but there's a car in the parking lot, so there must be someone home. I step up to the back door and test it, and sure enough, someone has turned the deadbolt and used it to hold the door open. It swings inward, and I hold it open for Kate with a curt nod to usher her in.

The interior is about what I expected, too. With all the lights on, the place's ambiance is ruined, and all the industrial interior design is on display, from the exposed brick wall to the exposed infrastructure in the ceiling to the dirty stage where shitty bands probably get up and belt out some off-tune covers on Fridays.

It's exactly my kind of place.

"Is anyone even here?" Kate asks.

"Yeah, and we're closed!" a voice shouts from the back, followed by some irritable-sounding footsteps. A tall man with a short beard and large, dark eyes steps out from a hallway leading to what I assume is the back offices, and I'm surprised when I recognize his face.

"Connor?" I say, raising an eyebrow and grinning. "You're kidding me, what are you doing here?"

"Breaker!" the big guy says, face brightening up. "Holy shit, man, how long has it been?"

Kate watches, perplexed, as the two of us approach each other and meet in a tight embrace that only lasts a moment before we check each other out and laugh.

"Too long, apparently," I say.

"Are you another one of Breaker's buddies?" Kate asks cautiously, glancing between us.

"Not the kind you're thinking of," I say hurriedly,

because I know Kate is worried that this guy is another one of the bikers from my club. "Connor's a friend I know though another friend. You get to know a lot of people on the club scene when you're riding between towns as much as we do."

Connor probably doesn't know the first thing about Kate's involvement with the club, and frankly, that's for the best. The guy is a bartender who bounces from place to place in the same area, and that means that he's the kind of guy everyone wants to be on the good side of. He has the laid-back personality for it, too, and all of that works to our advantage right now.

I never thought I'd be looking to Connor as a welcome advantage, but considering the past 36-ish hours we've spent not able to catch a single break, I'll take what I can get.

"Okay," Kate says, a little relieved. "Then, do you mind if I use your bathroom, Connor? The club's bathroom. You know what I mean."

"Yeah, sure thing," he says, nodding in the direction of the restrooms while I make my way over to the bar and lean back on it, crossing my arms and watching her go. Once the door shuts behind her, Connor looks to me with raised eyebrows and a knowing smile on his face.

"It's not what you think," I say, chuckling yet quiet enough that there's no chance Kate can hear me from the bathroom.

"Really? The way she looks at you, I think she might want it to be," he teases, and I roll my eyes. "Anyway, what's up? I don't remember you as the type to show up before opening. Everything okay?"

"We're looking for someone who was here two nights ago," I say. "A friend of Kate's. She was here too."

"I thought she looked kind of familiar," Connor says, nodding thoughtfully. "Can't say I remember any faces from two nights ago though, sorry."

"Not to put on any pressure, but we're struggling hard to find anything," I say, frowning.

"Okay, what did she look like?" he asks, crossing his arms.

"Blonde with curly hair, sounds like she was dressed for clubbing. Probably goes out like this a lot, but I don't think she comes here often. Probably looked out of place, like she belongs in the kind of bar that college kids spend time at and just ended up here."

"That… might be familiar, but I see a lot of girls like that, I've gotta be honest," he says, shaking his head. "There isn't exactly a lot to do in Stonedale, locals go wherever they can."

"She was with a guy she met here," Kate says suddenly, emerging from the bathroom and getting both our attention. "Tall guy with light hair that's kind of scruffy, blue eyes, ratty clothes, too much body spray. He had kind of a distinct smile, his mouth was kind of big."

My eyebrows go up, and I'm impressed by how much detail she can remember about her friend's date. It's not just impressive that she was able to memorize that much about him after seeing him once in a dark club. It shows that she was probably watching out for her friend, paying attention to the guy she was with in case he turned out to be dangerous.

It's a shame Moxie apparently didn't think to return the favor. I'm starting to get an idea of their dynamic, and it makes me sad to know Kate seems to be the type to give more than she gets out of her friendships. Maybe I'm just reading into things too much, but the kid has a good head on her shoulders, and I don't like knowing that she's not being treated well.

"Now *that* rings a bell," Connor says, stroking his beard.

"Yeah, actually, it does," I say, crossing my arms and meeting Connor's gaze. "Sounds a lot like Mitch Pratley."

"That's what I was thinking," Connor agrees, and Kate blinks a few times, looking between us.

"What does Mitch Pratley mean? Good or bad?" Kate asks, almost hesitant.

"Mitch is a groupie for my club," I say with a deep sigh. "He's a hanger-on. Groupies hang around us like remora on a shark because they all want to become prospects—that's someone who *could* be a member after getting vetted."

"So… Mitch is close to the club?" she asks. Her tone is remarkably calm in front of Connor, and I can't help but admire her for it. "Do you think he could hurt Moxie?"

"Hardly," I snort. "The guy's got spirit, but he's a punk, and his dad's a straight-laced judge to boot. Can't be bought. We won't touch him with a sixty-foot pole, and I think he knows it deep down."

"He couldn't hurt your friend," Connor agrees, shaking his head. "He's a pussy trying to act out for Daddy's attention. My guess is, he'll settle out when the judge sends him to some ivy league college. The worst your friend might have gotten is a disap-pointing night. But if you're looking for her and they were together, I can point you in the right direction."

"Really?" Kate asks, eyes widening.

"Easy," Connor says, pointing eastward. "You know that big place with the ugly statues out front people make fun of? That's Mitch's dad's house, and he bought his boy his own place right next door to the left. Orange sports car parked out front, can't miss it."

"He leaves it parked outside?" I ask, raising an eyebrow.

Connor just rolls his eyes in response, nodding, and we chuckle.

After a firm handshake and a few fond farewells, Kate and I leave, and I try to shake the thought that among all the other things I've come to know in this part of the country, I probably won't be seeing Connor ever again after this morning.

"So, you know the place we're headed to?" I ask as we drive down the road a few minutes later.

"Yeah, you can't miss this place," she says. "The guys in high school always had a running dare for each other to see if they'd be brave enough to egg the place. We all knew it was a judge's, though, so I don't think anyone ever went through with it."

Just a fifteen-minute drive later, we slowly roll by the manor in question. I have to admit, I can see why people wanted to egg this place. It features a circular driveway with the most obnoxious palm trees lining the place that I'd ever seen, wafting in the breeze like this was Bel Air or something, but the real kicker was not one, not two, but three separate gorilla statues that looked like they had been arranged in no particular order in the yard.

"I…" I stutter as I stared at the place.

"Yeah, I think they're like that so they look like they're 'in the wild' or something," Kate says.

"Holy shit," I chuckle as we pull to the next house over and come to a stop at the curb.

Sure enough, the orange sports car is sitting outside, and I look to Kate, who locks eyes with me.

"I can handle this," Kate says. "If this Mitch guy

answers the door, he'll react better to me than he will to you."

"I know you can handle it, but I can't let you go up there on your own," I say, shaking my head.

"Come on, you're not my dad," she protests, crossing her arms and narrowing her eyes at me.

"You wish," I say, winking at her as I open the driver's side door, and I watch the color flush to her cheeks as she gets out.

In truth, the main reason I want to go with her is because there's a small sliver of a chance word has gotten out about Kate. Mitch isn't capable of much, but on the off chance he heard about what happened and wants to impress Buzz, he might try something stupid, and I want to make sure I have Kate's back.

We approach the front door and ring the doorbell, and as we're standing uncomfortably outside, I notice Kate is still wearing my leather jacket just before the door opens.

Mitch stands there in sweatshorts and a sports team tee, blinking at us with a hung-over expression, but he brightens up at the sight of me.

"Oh shit, hey bro!" he says, lifting his hand to give me a high five, but I just give him a curt nod, and he plays off the gesture as if he was covering his mouth to cough.

At the same time, a short woman pokes her head out from behind Mitch, and a moment later, who I can only assume is Moxie steps out from behind him and waves to Kate with an excited look on her face.

"Oh my god, girl, where have you been?" she gushes as Kate rushes forward and hugs Moxie, to her surprise.

"Holy shit, Moxie," she breathes before stepping back. "What happened the other night? I'm so glad you're okay, I was worried sick! I… lost my phone," she says, glancing back at me briefly.

"It's no big deal, I've just been here," she says, nodding at Mitch affectionately. "Mitch, this is a friend of mine, Kate, I think they're just stopping by."

"Oh. Alright," Mitch says, nodding and glancing between me and Kate and trying to keep his cool. I had to admit, I wasn't the biggest fan of groupies. "Just uh, come hit me up if you want to play some video games or something, Breaker, yeah?"

I give the faintest shadow of a nod to get Mitch to beat it, and he vanishes into the house, leaving the three of us together.

"Is that what you ditched me in the fucking biker club for?" Kate whispers with a deadpan glare at Moxie, who shrugs in response.

"Looks like you did alright for yourself, sis," she says in her defense, smirking while giving me a long and blatant once-over. Kate's face reddens, and I can see the impulse in her to step between the two of us.

I can't help but chuckle, and Kate pinches the bridge of her nose.

"Kate's just had a long day," I say.

"I just had no idea if you were okay," she says, looking at Moxie with an exasperated look on her face.

"Well, I'm good, don't worry," Moxie says more sincerely. "I didn't think it was a big deal. You make it sound like something bad happened, is everything alright? Was there like a fight or something? Give me the details!"

"No, but-" Kate starts to say, and in an instant, I react.

My arm lunges out and wraps around Kate's waist, and I pull her close to me, pressing her hips to mine and forcing her to look up at me with wide, surprised eyes, so close that I can feel her breath on my face.

"It's not polite to share all our dirty details, sweetheart," I growl with a wicked smile, and her mouth falls open. She takes a breath to protest, but even though her friend is right there, I lean in and stop the words from coming from her mouth with a single, long kiss that takes her by utter surprise.

Because this is how it needs to be now. No telling. No stories. No connections. We're each other's dirty little secret now, and I'm going to make sure she keeps her mouth shut.

Personally.

Ugh, the time is passing so slowly, the clock on the wall in the breakroom at work might as well be turning counter-clockwise. I sigh and flop over into one of the cushy, stark-white mod chair in the lounge, staring up at the ceiling. I am so beyond bored. I feel like this day has lasted a thousand years. I usually do enjoy my job, but on days like this when there are no bookings, I feel restless and antsy. I cross my legs and lean back in the chair, swivel idly from side to side as I listen to the seconds ticking on the wall.

In the floor-length mirror across the room, meant for helping the masseuses to keep their uniform perfectly spotless and wrinkle-free, I gaze at my own reflection. In the past six years since I hightailed it out of my sleepy hometown of Stonedale, a lot has changed. In a lot of ways, I'm nothing like the shy, reserved, sheltered girl I used to be back then. I just passed my twenty-fourth birthday a couple months ago, bringing me closer and closer to what I'm dreading will become a quarter-life crisis.

I can't think of any other explanation for the way I have been feeling lately. I'm no longer content to waste long swaths of my days off curled up on my secondhand sofa in the tiny living room of my six-hundred-square-foot apartment, watching TV show reruns in my pajamas and ordering chicken lo mein delivered to my house. The weekends I used to spend traipsing happily through the endless stalls and vendors of the local Casper Flea Market have begun to lose some of their sheen.

Hell, even here at work I find myself zoning out and forgetting to keep up a calm conversation with my clients as I squirt warm, fragrant oil on their wound-up, tight muscles and use my small but dexterous hands to gently massage the pain and stress away. It used to be my favorite part of the job; just getting to interact with strangers on a personal level. In a lot of ways, being a masseuse feels kind of like how I imagine being a shrink must feel. People come to me in pain, under enormous stress, desperately looking for someone to coax their aching bodies back to life again. They come here in search of some relaxation, of two smooth, masterful hands to rub the pain away and two ears to listen to the bevy of complaints they've been lugging around like dead weight for weeks, months, even years.

Those were my most exciting bookings: the newbies.

I take such great joy in feeling years and years of built-up tension start to slowly melt away under my fingertips. It makes me feel powerful, like I possess some kind of magic that can help people find their lust for life once again. Maybe that's just my wild imagination blossoming in too many directions at once. Maybe it's a little romanticized. But at the end of the day, I have learned to really enjoy my job and its strange, unexpected little perks. Of course, the pay and the tips I often receive aren't half-bad either. But it's the personal connections I can make with my clients that keeps me coming back to the parlor to do it six days a week.

Still, even that magical feeling has been muted lately.

I've found myself strangely less interested in the personal anecdotes my customers share with me. My mind often just strikes out on its own, wandering far beyond the usual safe territory I've built up in my head to protect myself. After all, there are things in my past I am still too afraid to poke at just yet.

Maybe someday.

But not now. I should still just be grateful for the life I'm leading, especially considering how dramatically worse it could have turned out that fateful night six years ago.

As I sit here, wrapped up in my own thoughts, I am suddenly interrupted by the clack-clack-clack of sharp stiletto heels against the laminate wood flooring. I sit up straighter and try to look alive, thinking it might be my scowly manager, Rita, coming to tell me off for wasting time. Not that there is anything else to do right now anyway. But to my relief, it's not Rita who comes walking into the breakroom. It's my work-buddy Caitlyn, or Cat for short. We first bonded when I began working here two years ago and realized how similar our names are. Kate and Cat, two peas in one oil-slicked pod full of soft, New-Agey music and the potent scents of incense.

She's a little older than me, so I've kind of thought of her as my big sister, which has been a comfort to me since I had to cut off all contact with my own sisters, brothers, and parents years ago. She's more sarcastic and savvy about the world than I am, so the dynamic often fits.

"Hey girl. You look comfy," she remarks as she walks in, dressed almost identically to me except for the heels.

Our loosely-prescribed "uniform" here at the parlor is a white blouse and black pants, hair up in a neat bun to indicate cleanliness. But Caitlyn always wears those clunky heels, while I tend to just wear comfortable black flats. I have my reasons for not wearing heels. Some of that reasoning has to do with just wanting to be comfortable since I do spend pretty much all day on my feet at work, but I'd be lying if I didn't mention that part of the reason is just that I hate the idea of not being able to run fast.

In flats, I can cover a lot more distance in a much shorter window of time than if I wear high heels. And after the trauma that occurred in my life six years ago, I've never stopped expecting that I might have to run at any point. I just like to be prepared, that's all. Maybe it's paranoid of me to think that way, but oh well. Better safe than sexy, so the heels are a no-go for me.

"I'm bored out of my mind, Cat. Are you sure we don't have any last-second bookings for the day?" I sigh.

She chuckles as she pours herself a tiny cup of espresso from the machine. She glances over at me in amusement.

"Are you actually complaining about getting paid to do nothing?" Caitlyn points out.

"Maybe," I admit. "But think of all the tips we could be earning."

"Meh. It's been go-go-go for me all this week. I am totally down for a day of rest, as long as Rita doesn't come sniffing around to give us busy work or something," she says, wrinkling her nose as she takes a sip of hot coffee.

None of us particularly enjoy spending time with

Rita, on or off the clock. She isn't a bad person by any stretch of the imagination, but she can be a bit of a buzzkill.

"I get that. I guess I'm just worried," I confess quietly. "My rent is coming due next Monday and I'm worried I won't be able to pay it on time. I just had to replace the timing belt in my car so money's a little tight. I could definitely use some tips at the moment. And it's been so slow around here since Christmas four months ago. Don't we usually get busier in January since everybody's got all their New Year's resolutions to get fit and do self-care and all that?"

"I guess people have a different resolution this year," Caitlyn remarks.

She flops down in the chair beside me, pulling her long legs up to her chest as she sips her drink. I watch the curls of hot steam dancing up from the top of the mug for a moment. I must look utterly zoned out, because Caitlyn tilts her head to one side and waves her hand in front of my face.

"Hello? Earth to Kate," she says. "You look exhausted, girl."

"It's stress," I sigh. "It feels like I spend all my time working, and yet I still don't know if I'll be able to pay rent. What am I doing wrong here?"

"Pfft. That's just the economy we're working with these days," she laments, rolling her eyes. "But

I'll let you in on a little secret: get yourself a side hustle."

"Side-hustle?" I repeat dubiously. "When the hell do you find time for that?"

She giggles. "I believe it's called moonlighting. I work here during the day, but one or two nights a week, I work at this other place, too," she explains in a hushed tone.

I lean forward with interest. "What other place?" I whisper.

Caitlyn's eyes dart back and forth as though checking to make sure the coast is clear. Then she leans in and says, "It's just like this one, only it pays a lot more."

"Really?" I ask, wide-eyed. "Where is it? Can I apply there? Are they hiring?"

She laughs and sips her coffee. "Oh, trust me: they're always hiring. But it takes a special kind of person to work there. You have to be willing to, uh, bend some of the usual rules of massage therapy if you want to fit in there," she says vaguely.

"What rules are you bending?" I ask pointedly. I have a feeling I know where this is headed, and judging by the suggestive smirk on my friend's face, I'm correct.

"The one about, um, personal contact," she whispers. "You know how people are always making jokes about how we should start giving out happy endings?"

I blanch at the phrasing. "Yes. Why?"

"Well, you asked what rules I'm bending. There's your answer. I give happy endings. Not every time, but most of the time. And before you get all judgy, let me say this, too: I make beaucoup tips, girl," Caitlyn admits proudly.

"What kind of tips are we talking?" I press her.

"Let's just say you wouldn't be worrying about rent at all," she quips with a wink.

I find myself totally intrigued—and yes, a little grossed out—by her revelation. On the one hand, I know it's totally unprofessional and risky to do what she's doing. If Rita or anyone else here at the parlor ever finds out what Caitlyn's been doing at her other job, she'd be fired before she could even say a word in her own defense. But on the other hand, I could definitely use the extra cash, and I have to admit that the idea of injecting some much-needed excitement into my boring routine is tempting. It's just not my style, though. Never has been. I was never the wild one. In fact, after what happened six years ago, my former best friend Moxie and I broke off contact. I realized I simply didn't have anything in common with her anymore. She was always seeking out trouble, while I was busy covering my tracks and lying low. I still crave adventure, of course, but not like that.

I want a kind of measured and safe excitement. An adventure I can feel safe doing. But I can't do it on my own. I would need someone strong and protective to watch over me and rein me in. Someone like Breaker.

Despite the fact that I have spent a lot of time these past six years doing everything in my power to forget him, to not think about him, he has never disappeared from my thoughts completely. He's always been there, lurking in the shadowy back corners of my head, waiting for me to think about him openly again. I can still so vividly remember the way he kissed me, the sensation of his lips against mine. The way his hand pressed supportively at the small of my back. The way he brought me back home and acted like a true gentleman. Still, though, he's the reason I had to leave Stonedale and abandon everything I had ever known and loved.

He said he would always be watching me.

I don't know if I believe that now, though. It's been six years and I've never seen hide nor hair of him since then. Surely he's given up on me by now. I felt his presence, more like a ghost haunting me than anything tangible, at first. I did as I was told. I left Stonedale, drove three and a half hours away to Casper, where I enrolled in community college under a made-up last name. Luckily, I managed to fake the documentation needed to join the massage college. I graduated with a certification as a masseuse, and I've been working here ever since.

For a while, I was just elated to finally be independent and working. I was starting to leave my dark past behind me, thinking I could finally move on. But after a while, I just began to feel lonely. My friends and colleagues here always try to set me up with men, always urging me to try dating apps.

But the truth is, I have no interest in those men.

For better or worse, I'm still hooked on the shimmering ideal in my head: Breaker, the man who saved my life.

My kidnapper-turned-hero who haunts my every dream and slips into my every fantasy. He always told me that if I ever told a living soul about what he did for me, he would come back to get me.

Though at first his threat scared me, over time it has come to excite me. The idea of running into Breaker again, regardless of the circumstances, is enough to make my heart race faster. Especially now that I have more free time. Things have slowed down considerably at the parlor, and the hours for my volunteer position as a kinesiologist at the local hospital have recently been cut, in favor of taking on someone with further schooling than I have. The fact of the matter is that nowadays I have more time to think. More time to stew on life, on how things didn't turn out quite the way I hoped. And I'm not getting any younger. I want adventure.

"Hey," Caitlyn says suddenly, shaking me out of my contemplation. "You okay there?"

"Yeah, yeah. Of course. My bad. I guess I just zoned out again," I admit.

"You looked like you were a million miles away, Kate. What's going on? What's on your mind, girl?" she asks with genuine concern.

I bite my lip, afraid to answer truthfully. But no respectable lie comes to mind, and she's waiting for me to say something… so I just say it.

"Years ago, before I started working here, I had a run-in with a pretty dangerous crowd," I murmur, almost as though I'm in a trance as I stare blankly at the breakroom table.

"Okay. And what happened?" she coaxes me.

"They kidnapped me. I was just a kid then. Eighteen. They put me in a room by myself and wouldn't let me out. Then, the most amazing man I've ever met—he came to save me. He set me free. But sometimes, when I'm alone and awake in the middle of the night, all I can think about is how scared I am," I whisper.

"Scared of what?" Caitlyn asks.

I swallow hard. "That they'll come back to get me any day now."

BREAKER

I'm not the boy I was six years ago.

I sit at the head of a heavy wooden table in the room that serves as our clubhouse's meeting place, hand on my chin as I gaze at the map of Crook County, Wyoming spread out before me. My kutte hangs on my shoulders proudly, and our club's symbol is on my back like a king's jewels: a devil piercing a bleeding heart with a spear.

We are the Wyoming Heartbreakers, and I'm their prez.

The map in front of me is marked in red with dozens of circles, scribbled notes, and arrows. I'm sitting back, still as a statue, taking a deep breath as I survey what has become the little kingdom I've carved out for our members.

My members.

Bones sits to my right, and Ironside is on my left.

Big Daddy sits across from me, and even Skid sits beside him. After six long years, these men are the people I call my allies, even after everything we've been through. And goddamn, have we been through a lot.

After I dropped off Kate, I went into hiding. I had no other options. I showed my face enough to keep the pressure on Kate and make sure she did as I said, but other than that, the better part of a year consisted of getting all too acquainted with the inside of a safe house I rented with cash. From there, all I could do was plan. I watched the movements of Buzz's old club as best as I could, but that was challenging sometimes. I'm the man who killed his son, and he wasn't about to let that go unanswered.

But once the energy for the hunt for me fizzled out, my old comrades showed their true colors, and for once, that was a good thing.

They split up.

It didn't happen all at once. Bones was the first one I got a hold of. Caught him in a motel halfway to Laramie and held him at gunpoint while he explained that Buzz had sent him out to find a girl for the strip club, but that his plan had been just to ride away and never look back. His story checked out. He had supplies with him, and he had always been a bad liar. I believed him and gave him an alternative: join my club.

Bones filled me in on the real situation back at

the old warehouse: not everyone was on board with Buzz's plan to get involved in sex trafficking. In fact, none of the ranking guys liked that idea, and Buzz was just the first one to have hit the road. They had all joined in the hunt for me because all they knew was that suddenly, I'd killed Roadster. Hell, for all they knew, we might have just gotten into a drunken fight and I'd killed him on accident.

He was half-right, I had to give him that.

Buzz tried to shut down the rumor that I'd kidnapped the girl because I wasn't down to start pimping sex slaves. He failed, and that was bad for him. I was a symbol of rebellion. I was proof that the members could defy him and get away with it. Ironside was the next most influential member who filled the power vacuum I left, so he was the next one to contact.

He was easy to recruit. He had always been a straightforward man, so we figured the straightforward approach was the easiest. The look on his face when we just showed up at his front door like a couple of salesmen was priceless. He had his bags packed within an hour.

Big Daddy looked like he was going to be trickier, but he sought us out. Tailed us for miles before catching up at a diner on the highway and hashing things out over a few coffees and orders of fried chicken. The man can eat, there's no question about that.

Skid still has a lot to learn, but he came to us by pure chance. Of all places, we rode past him outside a church in Casper, where he wasn't even wearing the old kutte. I pulled him aside and offered him the chance to do something that wouldn't weigh on his conscience so much. He was more than eager to jump horses and ride with us.

And I've gotta say, now that I'm calling the shots, things have been going well.

Crook County has been good to us, and we're based out of some prime real estate in a town called Pine Haven. Our clubhouse is situated underground, under a modest establishment above that we have a good arrangement with. We don't get bothered by strangers, we're well connected to the highways, and best of all, the local cops recognize that we're doing a better job at serving justice than most of them ever could.

That means they've been willing to cooperate.

I stand up slowly and look around at all the men gathered before me with a hard gaze.

"I want to hear your version of a full report," I say, "from you, Bones. Tell me how things got out of hand. From the start, step by step, and then *I'll* tell you whether the cops are overreacting."

"We started with what you gave us in the last meeting," Bones says, leaning forward. "One of our sets of eyes in town saw Ted James at a white table-cloth dinner with a guy we know to be a fracking lobbyist. They want to start fracking near Devil's Tower, and they're trying to climb in bed with small time politicians like Ted James."

"Young councilman of a town of less than two thousand, he's probably looking for low hanging fruit like that," I agree, nodding. "He doesn't have much of a track record, but the cops we have in pocket back up their theory that he's liable to try this kind of thing."

"We looked into the agenda for the next town council meeting and found that it's up for discussion," Bones goes on. "Ted James himself wasn't going to bring it up in person, he's smarter than that. He had a bought citizen put it forward, probably so that he could jump on it and spin it to the others like a sales pitch."

"A good boost to the local economy would look good if he wants to make a bid for mayor next election," Ironside adds, nodding in agreement.

"Never trust a man with two first names," I sigh, shaking my head. "Alright, so we're caught up to where Big Daddy, Bones, and Ironside busted into the council meeting. Give me the play by play."

"Ironside took the lead, Big Daddy had our rear," Bones says as the other two look on, knowing better than to try to talk over each other. "We'd been expecting to show up, make our presence known, maybe hoot and holler a little to disrupt things. What we didn't know was that Ted had armed security guards on the premises, and they were looking out for us."

"What does that mean?" I ask, drilling Bones for every detail I can get."

"Twice as many guys as usual, and they moved on us too fast not to have been prepped beforehand,' Bones says confidently. "I'd stake my life on it. Ted knew we'd be coming."

"So, what, was there a gunfight in the town council chambers?" I ask.

"No shots fired," Bones says quickly. "Guess Ted couldn't afford real-ass bodyguards, because the armed guards just rushed us and tried to intimidate us out. I don't even think any of them pulled their guns out. Well, they tried to after Ironside dropped the first one to come too close to us."

"I wasn't about to get escorted off the premises," Ironside growls.

"No, that was good," I say, nodding. "It would have made us look weak at a meeting like that. What next?"

"A brawl that only lasted a few seconds," Bones says. "Ironside took down another guy, and Big Daddy got to the other two before I could, so I watched the exit. The uh, attendees were a little excited at that point, so instead of taking a seat we decided to shout at Ted to keep his hands off the oil money, and we beat it. That was it. No deaths, maybe a concussion or two at worst. Don't think the security guards were even locals."

I nod solemnly, staring at the map for a few moments as I process my thoughts.

"The boys in blue probably wanted a quieter job, but it sounds like we got our message across. It might even work to our advantage that we made such a forceful show. It'll prove that we've got more muscle than anything the likes of Ted can pull out of his ass, and that means something, even if it's basic. I'll go with your word and tell the cops they're exaggerating, but let's do some more intel gathering in the future, keep ourselves from getting blindsided like that in the future. You did good, but all it would have taken for things to go south is for one of those guards to pull a gun. And I don't think we've heard the last of this."

"That's the least of our problems right now, Prez," Big Daddy speaks up, and I raise an eyebrow at him as he puts a finger on the map not far from Crook County's borders. "Table Rock Buzzsaws have been spotted in Gilette."

My jaw sets, and I stare long and hard at the map. The Buzzsaws are the new incarnation of the old MC that Buzz pulled together after half his damn club jumped ship to ride with me instead. They've been pushing north and east hard over the past couple of years, and I know exactly why.

Buzz hasn't forgotten me anymore than I've

forgotten the way Roadster's skull felt on my brass knuckles when I killed him.

"We know they have a presence in Buffalo," Big Daddy goes on, "but we don't know if they've got a foothold in Gilette yet. But it's the same pattern as when they pushed into Buffalo. Prez, I hate to say it, but they'll be in Crook County before much longer. I know we've got to keep the locals on our side, but Buzz is a problem we'll have to deal with before it deals with us."

"You're right," I agree, nodding. "Tell me, have you heard anything from Cheyenne?"

"They've stayed clear so far, or they're being careful about it," Big Daddy says. "Or maybe they haven't gotten that far southeast yet. But they're closing in. They're already in Casper."

"I know," I murmur with the faintest undertone of a growl under my breath. "That's the problem."

Kate is in Cheyenne.

I've been keeping an eye on her for all these years, probably more than I need to. I have an informant in Cheyenne keeping tabs on her—and keeping her phone bugged—but I go myself as often as I can. That ghost from my past has been burning bright as her auburn hair in my mind ever since we parted ways all that time ago. She hasn't seen me in that time, but I've seen her. I'm watching her every step, because she's the biggest walking liability I've ever let go free.

If she plays her cards right, she could cause a hell of a lot of trouble for me and my club. She might even be able to bring us down. She's grown into an incredible woman, and I wouldn't put anything past her, but I can't read her mind, even if I can keep an eye on her texts.

"Prez, I know I sound like a broken record," Big Daddy says as I cross my arms, anticipating what he's about to say. "But we need to bring Kate in."

"She hasn't said a word, and you know that," I say firmly. "Nothing's changed since the last time we had this conversation."

"The hell it hasn't," Big Daddy retorts, and I raise my eyebrows at the challenge. "The Buzzsaws are closer than ever to Cheyenne. If Buzz is avoiding it, he might know she's there, and if he knows, he knows she's a liability. You're looking out for her, but Buzz might just kill her. If not that, then the second she gets a whiff of their bikes in her territory, she might get scared and go to the cops. And you know as well as I do, we don't have jack shit in Cheyenne."

"I'm not bringing her in," I repeat, shaking my head. "She's got a life, and she's held up her side of our bargain. Six years, and I've kept a closer eye on her than I've kept on any of you, you know that."

"All too well, Prez," says Big Daddy, minding his tone a little more this time and nodding slowly. "I know you care about… this," he says carefully.

"Look, all I'm saying is, I know how hard it can be to keep your head clear when there's a woman involved."

"If you want to say something, say it," I say, leaning forward on the table and glaring at Big Daddy with a steely gaze that he meets head-on.

Our eyes are locked for a few long moments, and inside, as angry as I am, I know he isn't talking out of jealousy or pettiness. He's a good man I'd trust with my life. But I know what I'm doing, and I'm not letting anyone put Kate in danger, much less myself.

Before either of us can break the silence, my phone on the table buzzes. I look down at it briefly before snatching it up and walking away from the table without a glance back.

"Meeting adjourned," I growl, and I head to my room.

I stay in a comfortable apartment connected to our clubhouse, which I imagine was a proprietor's place long ago. It's effectively a cozy one-bedroom, which is practically a palace compared to what I'm used to. Motorcycle and band posters litter the walls, taking up almost as much space as there is to take up, and wherever those aren't, I have pictures of home hanging. It's a small touch to a place I'm not holed up at all the time, and it makes it feel like my own little slice of home.

I open my phone to check the notification, and my heart drops. The bug I have on Kate's phone is set up to notify me whenever certain trigger words get texted. In case she's thinking about talking to anyone about what happened or even about me, I'll be the second person to know. And she just used one of those words:

Breaker.

"I've never known a girl quite like you, Katherine, and I don't think I ever will again if you walk out that door," declares the handsome man with the sorrowful face. He has his hands clasped in front of his chest, both clear blue eyes pleading and shimmering with that could almost be genuine, bespoke human tears if I didn't know any better.

"Damn. He's a good actor," I murmur to myself as I reach my hand into the bowl of salty, buttery popcorn mixed with chocolates and nuts in my lap.

It's my favorite movie-bingeing snack. Salty and sweet. Crunchy and sinful. I know it's a bad habit but I can't help it. I try to eat healthy for the most part. When I pack my lunch to take to the parlor with me every day, it usually consists of some raw baby carrots or celery with a tiny container of hummus or a mustardy dipping sauce, plus some low-fat cottage cheese and jam. Caitlyn, my coworker, is always teasing me for my boring goody-two-shoes lunches, especially compared to my coworkers who usually pick up Chinese takeout or pizza for lunch. But little does she know, I have a raging sweet tooth, too. At work I manage to restrain myself, but once I clock out for the day and head home? All bets are off. No rabbit food to speak of. Oh well. I work awfully hard at the parlor and I can logic myself into justifying my comfort food favorites. Sometimes a girl just needs a cozy night in on her couch with yummy, unhealthy snacks and an overly dramatic romance movie.

And if there's a glass of wine thrown into the mix, well, that's good, too.

I lean forward to pick up my wine glass from the little secondhand coffee table in front of my thrift-shop sofa. I give the white wine a subtle sniff before sipping it, letting the fruity, floral notes pass over me. I sigh with delight as the sweet, refreshing Riesling tingles down through my body. At the end of a long day, this is exactly what I need to loosen me up and relieve some of the crazy tension. It's funny—I spend all day massaging my clients and reducing their stress, but I don't have the power to do that for myself. And while some of my coworkers are less inhibited than I am and will gladly book sessions with fellow masseuses, I have always been too timid and awkward to do that. I don't want to have to look across the big mahogany table at a board meeting and gaze into the eyes of someone who just had their bare, oiled-up hands sliding around on my naked body. That seems like a boundary I just simply don't want to cross. Maybe that makes me a bit of a prude, but oh well. That's just the way I am. I'm particular about who I let close enough, who I allow access to my thoughts and feelings and worries.

When you've been lowkey on the run for six years, you tend to be a little paranoid from time to time. That just comes with the territory.

A swell of dramatic violin and piano music floats out of the television speakers, distracting me from my thoughts and back to the screen in front of me. Now, Mr. Handsome Blue Eyes is kneeling down on the rocky edge of a cliff in front of the object of his desire, a stunningly gorgeous woman named Katherine. Her long, wavy blonde hair billows and whips around romantically in the wind. I squint at the screen, trying to figure out if they actually had a budget that would include filming on location or if this is just one hell of a convincing sound stage. After all, this isn't some high-dollar, elaborate, Oscar-bait blockbuster. It's a made-for-TV movie like the ones my mom used to obsessively watch in the evening after she assumed all five kids had drifted off to sleep. I think it was kind of her guilty pleasure, her way to unwind after a thirteen-hour shift at the hospital. Poor Mom. She used to come home so late at night, miss dinner, and come in smelling like sterile disinfectant and disease. I have a lot of respect for nurses. It's hard, slogging work much of the time, and god knows they don't get paid enough to do it all. Watching my mother struggle all the time was definitely a life lesson for me.

Find a job you can tolerate, and try not to make it your entire life.

Of course, ever since moving to Casper, I've had some difficulty maintaining a balance between work and play. Mostly because I don't know enough people locally to have much fun during my 'play' hours. For the first year or so of living here after being forced to flee my hometown of Stonedale at the tender age of eighteen, I was simply too paranoid to make friends. I was constantly looking over my shoulder, carrying a pocket knife in parking lots at night just on the off chance I needed to protect myself. Every step I took, I feared that the mysterious but terrifying 'Prez' would be right behind me, ready to slip a rucksack over my head and drag me off to some windowless white van where he could do whatever he wanted with me. I have a feeling that a guy like the Prez isn't the type to forgive and forget. I know he is holding a grudge against me. After all, I'm the one that got away.

"When you disappeared that night, I assumed I would never see you again," laments the beautiful blonde actress on the screen.

The handsome actor shakes his head vehemently and reaches up to clasp her hands.

"I could never stay away for long. I'm addicted to you, Katherine. I need you. Now and forever. I won't let go. I won't move on. You're the only one for me," he begs.

The camera zooms in on his face just as one perfect, fat, crystalline tear squeezes out of his eye and rolls down his cheek. I pop another handful of candy and nuts into my mouth, staring at the screen intently. I know it's cheesy, but I have a soft spot for these flicks. Maybe it's because of my mom. Or maybe it's just a weird genetic predisposition to love romance movies. Who knows? Either way, I find myself disappointed that the movie is almost over.

"Oh, Alexander! You know just what to say!" exclaims the blonde woman. She flings her arms open and the guy called Alexander jumps to his feet. He wraps his strong arms around her and spins her around right there on the precipice of the cliff, her poufy dress swaying in the breeze. He sets her back down and cups her face lovingly, gazing deeply into her eyes.

"Wow. That's some serious chemistry," I remark out loud to nobody but myself.

The couple embraces and kisses each other very chastely, their mouths not even slightly open. Still, it's enough to get my heart racing. These days, I'm kind of existing on a hair trigger for romance and excitement. I get so little of it in my day-to-day life that even a soft, pure kiss between actors on a screen can get the adrenaline pumping.

Wow. Maybe I *am* a prude.

I watch as the ending of the movie unfolds—a big, elaborate white wedding with hundreds of guests (who even knows that number of people?). Complete with thousands of flowers and bows and course after course of the most delicious, aesthetically pleasing food. A cake towering high with five tiers, topped with the usual pair of bride and groom figurines holding hands. Everyone is happy. Everyone is smiling. The whole family is there, and yet there's no drama to speak of. Everybody is just supportive and loving and having a good time. I have a feeling that's never how it works out in real life. I feel a pang of sadness, realizing for the umpteenth time that I will probably never get to experience something like the opulent affair going on in front of me. I have not spoken to my family in six years and to be honest, I don't know if they have even been looking for me. After all my parents do have two other daughters and two sons besides me.

Maybe they just think of me as an ungrateful runaway, someone who betrayed the family by disappearing into thin air. It breaks my heart to think of it that way but if there's anything that I have learned over the past six years on my own, it's that you can't depend on anybody. Only yourself.

The scene on the TV in front of me shows all of the hundreds of guests dancing and laughing to a live band deep into the night. The happy couple shares a moonlit kiss and then it fades to the credits. I find myself strangely unsatisfied by the ending. It was too routine. Too expected. I need a little bit more excitement than that, personally.

With a heavy sigh, I grab the remote control and flip to a different channel, hoping to find something a little more compelling. I search through the channels until I land on something that looks promising. My heart skips a beat. There are motorcycles rumbling onscreen. All of the characters standing around are dressed like typical bikers. And one of them, I can't help but notice, looks a hell of a lot like Breaker. Incredibly handsome in a rugged sort of way. Rough around the edges just how I like it. He's wearing a plain white T-shirt loosely tucked into his black jeans which are loosely cuffed at the bottoms to show off his big, heavy riding boots. I can see the muscle rippling underneath the fabric of his clothing and it makes my heart beat just a little bit faster. I can't help but be reminded of the fateful night six years ago when I ended up on the back of a motor-cycle, first when I was drugged and kidnapped by that guy. And second, when I was rescued by the mysterious and sexy man I know only as Breaker. It's strange; sometimes I feel as though he might be close by. Like I can feel him, his raw and powerful energy in the air. Sometimes when I go out to the grocery store or to work, I can't help but look around for him as though I'm going to suddenly see his face in the crowd. I am still conflicted on whether or not I *want* to see him again.

God knows I could use a little excitement. But Breaker? He could be a little bit more exciting than I need.

On the screen, the sexy biker slips an arm around the girl with shiny brown hair, pulling her close. With a mischievous grin, he leans in and presses a decidedly not-chaste kiss to her lips. Open-mouthed. Passionate. Forceful. I can feel my body heating up just watching it. The romance movie earlier made me feel all mushy and gushy inside, but this motorcycle show is really revving my engine. I can almost put myself in the place of that pretty brunette. I imagine Breaker putting his arms around me, holding me against his hard, muscular body. I still so vividly remember the way he kissed me that day. I can still taste him, if I think hard about it.

I lick my lips, watching the screen with rapt attention as the biker pins his brunette girlfriend against a brick wall. He wedges a leg between her thighs and ruts against her, both of them grunting and moaning with desire. Against my better judgement, I slowly let my hand slip down my body, sliding underneath my silky turquoise pajama pants to my slick flower beneath the fabric. I bite my lip as my fingertips start to gently circle and massage my clit, exhilaration pumping through my whole body.

Outside, I swear I can hear the telltale rumble of a motorcycle engine. It certainly isn't coming from the TV. But I must be imagining it, right? What are the chances?

Either way, it turns me on even more. I roll my hips, working my clit until I'm nearly dangling over the edge of no return. It feels so good, and it's so easy to imagine that it's Breaker touching me like this. I can picture his dark eyes gazing into mine as his hands work their magic on my body. I close my eyes, losing myself to the steady waves of pleasure and the fantasy in my mind. The engine revs louder and more aggressively, the sound getting tougher and more intense in tandem with my mounting pleasure. I can almost smell Breaker's masculine, musky scent. I can feel and smell the leather. The fuel. The desperation between us as his hands grope my body and I give myself up to him. I can feel his rock-hard abs and his rough, stubbly jawline as he kisses me deeply. My fingers press harder against my sensitive clit and I let out a whimper of bliss.

This is so bad. It's so wrong. I shouldn't be thinking of Breaker this way. But I'm just so starved for attention, for touch. And I can't think of anyone I desire more than him. I fear him almost as much as I lust for him. It's foolish, but I can't help it. He weaves his way into my every sex dream, my every vivid fantasy. I want him now even more than I did six years ago. I just can't seem to shake my desire for the gruff, mysterious stranger who saved my life and changed its trajectory forever.

I rub tighter and harder circles around my clit, rocking and rolling my hips. The bowl of snacks tumbles and spills all over the floor but I don't care. Right now, all that matters to me is chasing that sensual high.

To my dismay, the sexy TV show cuts to commercial, but then it hits me that the motorcycle engine is still rumbling outside. In fact, it's getting louder, getting more intense along with the building tension in my body. It's getting so close now, and so am I. But then, before I can come, it stops suddenly. I sigh with disappointment, my climax dissipating before I can reach it. Now it's just curiosity that has me listening for the motorcycle outside. Suddenly, I'm overcome with the need to look outside and see it with my own eyes. So, I get off the couch and wander over to the window, peering down at the street below.

"Oh my god. No. No way," I gasp.

My heart pounds like crazy and adrenaline flows through my frame. There's a biker out there. A familiar one with a shiny new bike. I would recognize him anywhere, even six years later.

It's Breaker, and he's gazing straight up at me as though he knows exactly which apartment is mine. As if he's known it along.

feel electricity crackling through my body as those green eyes lock onto me for the first time in six long years. It feels like a lifetime ago that I first saw those scared, shimmering eyes looking out at me from the inside of that shed back at Buzz's old place. It may as well have been. The second thought in my mind is how she's changed over the years, what kind of person this girl has become.

The first thought on my mind is what she was doing that has her blushing so furiously.

I've seen her plenty of times, of course. I've watched her, both in person and from afar. I've seen her at cafes and out shopping in the city. I've followed her to job interviews and meetups with friends alike. I've always kept my distance, always stayed a few steps away, just enough to stay out of sight. She doesn't know just how well I know her life.

I have to stay close to her. If I lost track of her, she would be a far bigger liability than Buzz could ever be. And I bet she knows that. I've gotten to see just how smart she is over the years. I could sense it when we were together, like an aura, but I've gotten to see it firsthand.

Watching her is one thing. My eyes have devoured her silhouette for years, watching her move, laugh, frown, and I know her maybe better than I even know myself. I've even been so close that I can see the whites of her eyes.

Having those eyes turned on me is another thing entirely.

The electricity in the air isn't just from the gaze we share from a distance. Thunder claps overhead, and I glance up at the gray skies. A springtime storm is threatening to burst through the churning mass of clouds overhead, and I lower my eyes back to Kate and smile at her. It's so similar yet so different from the first time we saw each other through the rain six years ago.

I park my bike and wink up at her when I see her in the window again before she darts out of sight. Just as the first couple of drops of rain patter against my forehead, I stride inside the apartment building and ride the elevator up to her floor. I know exactly which apartment she lives in, of course. This isn't the first time I've been outside her apartment.

It's just the first time I've let myself be seen.

When I reach her apartment door, I have to admit, my heart is pounding hard. This moment has played through my head many a time. It's funny, it really isn't something I should have ever had reason to do. If all had gone according to plan, I'd never have to visit Kate as long as either of us lived. But regardless, I've done it a hundred times in my mind.

I've even thought about how easy it would be to have a key made or pick the lock and come in by force if I needed to. But Kate is smarter than that, I'd like to think. It wouldn't come to that unless she wanted it to.

My fist bangs on the door, and moments later, it opens it. Kate stands there in her pajamas, blushing even more furiously than when I saw her from the window. There's fear on her face, but so many other emotions stewing just under the surface, like she can't decide what she wants to show me. Poor little thing doesn't know how easily I can read her.

In storm of feelings battling for dominance behind those green eyes, I can see surprise… but not that much surprise. She wasn't expecting to see me tonight, but she has the look of someone gazing at an old friend. Maybe even an old lover. Has she been thinking about me?

"You're here," she breathes, her voice shaking.

"I warned you," I say, stepping forward and putting a hand on the doorframe. Her eyes widen, and she steps back. There's nobody else in the apartment hallway, and I'd rather not have witnesses to our little rendezvous, so I follow her in. She steadily moves away from me, and I shut the door behind me while my glare locks onto her.

"What do you want?" she says in a trembling voice, swallowing hard.

"Figured you would have grabbed a knife by now," I say, chuckling darkly. "You smell like sex. Am I interrupting something?"

"W-what? No! How did you-"

"That's none of your business, little girl," I growl as I close the distance between us with slow, measured steps, never breaking eye contact. "I warned you not to talk. Not to breathe my name to anyone. Who was it, hm?"

She lets me stalk up to her, which surprises me so much that I keep an eye out for an actual hidden knife, something she might be hiding from me. But her feet seem rooted in place, and even though her face is red and her chest is rising and falling with quick, terrified breaths, she isn't retreating from me.

I've made plenty of "house calls" in my time, but I've never had someone react quite like this.

"You're as pretty as you were back then, you know that?" I say as I loom over her. I reach down and take her chin in my thumb and forefinger, and touching her skin again is like a bolt of lightning through my body.

She senses it too. There's an energy in her that I recognize now, like a magnetic pull to me that I find *very* interesting. I narrow my eyes at her and turn her head, but those green eyes are locked onto mine.

"You're quiet," I remark. "Nothing to say? Gonna try to explain yourself? Is this reunion not going the way you hoped it would?"

"From you?" she breathes, an unmistakable edge of defiance in her tone that sends shivers down my spine. "No, it's going about like I expected."

A grin spreads across my face. This is too much to be real. The girl who's haunted my every dream for the past six years is right here in my grasp, and I'm finding that the tension I've felt building up in my body all this time doesn't just remember me. I recognize the feeling in the air, the energy barely held together just under the surface of her soft skin.

"Thought about it, have you?" I say, reaching down and taking one of her small, fragile hands in me larger and rougher one. I bring her fingers up to my lips, and I smell her pussy on them. Her mouth falls open as I simply breathe in instead of kissing them, then wrap my hand around them and give them a gentle squeeze. "Then tell me what I do next in this little fantasy of yours?"

She glares at me defiantly for what feels like an eternity, and her jaw tightens. She looks poised to find her backbone and try to kick me out of the house. I'd love to see her try that, and I honestly don't know if she really has it in her. She seems to be trembling one moment, rebellious the next, and hungry for me all throughout.

"Seems like I should have come in for a visit a long time ago, Kate," I say. "Maybe if I'd given you a little attention sooner, you wouldn't be acting out like this."

"What are you really here for, Breaker?" she asks in a voice just barely above a whisper.

"You," I answer.

My hand grasps her auburn hair, pulls it back, and presents her lips for me to lean down and kiss. Her body tenses up as our lips meet, but immediately, she starts to melt into my grasp. Her lips are warm, soft, and more delicious than I remember. I start to walk her back, further down the hall, and I stop only when we bump against a wall. I pin her to it and ravish her with kisses, breaking away from her lips to attack her neck and squeeze her hips.

She gasps, and I think she's about to push me away for a moment, but she doesn't. I can feel her heart racing, and I feel the heat radiating off her face, but it all spurs me on faster.

Finally, I feel her hands on my sides, and her fingers curl inward. My heart roars in victory as she lets herself indulge in my body. Her fingertips feel the hardened muscles under my kutte and my white t-shirt that I've worked so hard to hone over the years. I've earned my strength in more than my share of fights, and I've made my body this way through hard work and putting my life on the line.

"Like what you feel, little girl?" I whisper in a rough husk in her ear as I press my body against hers.

"Fuck," is all she manages to breathe, but even as she says it, her hands roam over my body, exploring me and memorizing the hardness of my torso. Her fingertips go past my belt and around to my tight ass, and I tear myself from her neck to look down at her with a wicked smile.

"Language," I tease, pushing my hips into her. I know she can feel my thick cock between her legs, and when I see the look on her face, it makes it throb even harder against her.

She's defiant, that much is obvious, but the blush in her cheeks and the way she bites her lip paint a very different story. I can't forget that I'm here for business, but both of us know this can't be all it's about. The only question is whether she'll admit that too.

"How long have you been watching me?" she asks, almost afraid to know the answer.

"I never stopped," I growl, squeezing her hips possessively, and letting one of my hands move around to her ass to squeeze it. "I've watched every little step you've been taking, sweetheart. Had to make sure you were being a good girl. And you have, until now. And I think you need to be reminded that I'm always watching."

"You've been stalking me," she breathes, and I tighten my grip on her ass.

"I think a reminder is exactly what you need tonight," I growl, and I feel the goosebumps on her arms. "Is that what you've been craving? I think it's been on your mind before I even got here. I've been honorable, Kate, I really have. And I've been more damn patient than you'll ever realize, because you're a hell of a prize to keep my hands off," I snarl, running my hands up and down her sides. "But you're giving me no choice."

She swallows.

"What are you going to do to me?" she asks, and her tone is so vulnerable yet so morbidly curious and ashamed of itself that I can't help but feel my blood run hot.

"I have to keep you under lock and key now," I say. "You've been one big walking liability for years, and I wanted to let you walk free, but those days are over. And now, I have to make you mine."

"Then prove it."

Kate seems to have a knack for finding the three magic words that I'm least expecting her to say, and she delivered those without missing a beat. She looks surprised that they came from her, but again…

not *too* surprised. And a direct challenge like that is something I simply can't ignore.

I lift her up and over my shoulder, ignoring her yelp of terror as I hold her legs together and carry her down the hallway. It doesn't take me long to find her bedroom, and I slide her off my shoulder, tending to her gentle squirming by sitting down on the bed with her and wrapping her in an embrace until my lips can find hers.

I sense anger in her kiss, but I only feel that through the white-hot energy between us. She grips my kutte and uses it to pull herself closer to me. My hands touch every part of her they can find, and through the soft, sheer fabric, the sensation of her body makes my cock plead for release.

"I like you, sweetheart, but I can't have you defying me like this," I growl. "How am I supposed to trust you if you go doing things like this? You're not giving me a choice."

"I can be good," she breathes, shuddering to hear herself say those words.

"Show me," I command her.

Her eyes flit down to the bulge in my jeans, then back up to my eyes, and I know what's on her mind. My lip curls, and I let out a rumbling chuckle from deep in my chest.

"On your knees," I order.

She nods feverishly, sliding down onto her knees at

the foot of the bed, and I take hold of her hair as she reaches forward and undoes my belt. I watch her carefully, making sure she isn't going to do anything stupid like hit me with it or try to run while I'm exposed. She's either a very good actress or really does want everything she's toying with, and if she does, she wants it *bad*.

Her hands work my pants open in a matter of seconds, but she almost hesitates before letting my cock spring out, as if she doesn't know if she was ready for this moment. But she pushes ahead, and her mouth falls open at the sight of my exposed girth.

My cock is thick and fully erect when she lays eyes on it, every inch of it bulging and desperate for release. My heavy balls are ready to give all they have to her, and when she licks her lips, my cock pulses with desire.

She looks up at me with a hazy, almost dreamlike gaze, as if she's trying to decide if this is real or not. I stroke her hair affectionately as she brings her lips to my cock and kisses it experimentally. As soon as she has confirmed that it's as solid as anything else, her hesitation evaporates.

She opens her mouth and takes my crown into it, and the moan she releases sends a ripple of warmth up my entire body. I grip the sheets with one hand and stroke her hair with the other as I feel her tongue pushing against me.

"More," I order her, tightening my grip on her

hair. Obediently, she takes more of my cock into her mouth with a soft whimper. Her tongue moves up and down my shaft ravenously, and the energy behind it isn't fear.

Kate must have wanted this as long as I have… maybe longer.

"You didn't think I'd go easy on you, did you?" my voice rumbles in the darkness of the bedroom. "When I say I'm taking your freedom, girl, I mean it. I gave it back to you, and you misbehaved."

She murmurs into my cock, but it doesn't stop her or even slow her down. She moves her lips up and down my shaft with a growing hunger every second.

"Feel my balls," I tell her. "Feel how heavy they are. And don't you slow down, sweetheart."

She brings a hand to my heavy sack and feels its weight, and I hear her give a moan of deeply ashamed pleasure as I give her hair a gentle tug to remind her that I'm holding the reins, nearly literally.

"That's for you," I growl, feeling goosebumps again. "All for you, if you work for it hard enough. I'm going to show you the consequences of your actions, Kate."

I'm in complete control of her, but I find myself surprised by her skill. She hasn't seen anyone in the time that we've been apart, not like this, but she's handling herself as if we never left. Her tongue gets to know my cock easily, and as soon as it does, it's like they were made for each other. I want to keep her bound to me like this all night, but I'm not letting her get me off before I teach her a lesson.

Just as I release a little precum for her to taste, I tighten my grip on her hair and start to pull her back. She fights it at first, and she tries to put her hands on my hips, but I pull more firmly.

"Stand up," I command her.

It's time to show Kate what happens to defiant little girls like her.

"I said stand up," Breaker growls.

I peer up at him with wide eyes, licking my lips. I can taste his potent flavor on my tongue still and it turns me on beyond belief. I don't want to give up yet. I can't get enough of his cock in my mouth, the way his thickness stretches out my cheeks and brushes ticklishly against the back of my throat. My mouth waters for it. I don't want to stop. But judging from the glowering look on Breaker's face, I had better do as I'm told unless I want to suffer the consequences.

Although, truth be told, I'm kind of turned on by the prospect of 'consequences' too.

Slowly, obediently, I rise up to my feet. I stand in front of Breaker, utterly at his beck and call, totally beholden to his desires. I have never felt so sexy, so desirable. I just want to be everything he needs me to be. I will gladly bend over backward to give him the pleasure he deserves. I wait expectantly for his next demand.

"Do you know why I made you stop?" he asks sharply.

I feel a rosy blush creep across my cheeks and I shake my head.

"No. I don't understand," I answer softly.

"It's because I'm not finished with you yet," Breaker hisses.

He reaches up to take my chin delicately in his hand, holding me in place. A shiver of lust runs down my spine at his touch. He gazes into my eyes, making my heart race like crazy. I'm totally locked into his every word, his every move. I'm intoxicated. My head clouded with need.

"What are you going to do with me?" I murmur.

He smirks and traces his thumb lightly over my full bottom lip. I can't resist the urge to softly kiss it, which makes the fire in his eyes blaze even brighter.

"I am going to take you exactly the way I want to, Kate," he snarls. "I'm going to claim you and make you all mine. Do you understand?"

The answer is yes and no. But I know better than to question him now.

I nod my head. "Yes, Breaker. I understand," I reply in a timid voice.

"Good," he says, leaning back. "Now take off your clothes for me, little girl."

The flush spreads from my cheeks down my neck and chest as I hesitantly do what he asks of me. One might think that with my job as a masseuse, I'd be more comfortable with nudity. But the truth is, I'm only accustomed to being the clothed one. I can't recall ever being naked in front of another living soul since reaching adulthood. I certainly have not shown my body to a man like Breaker. But he's right: I am his. I always have been, ever since we first met six years ago. There's no use resisting. This is everything I've been too afraid to admit I want.

I gradually peel off each article of clothing individually, careful to avert my gaze at first for modesty's sake. That is, until Breaker commands, "Look at me, Kate."

My lashes flutter as I raise my glance to meet his eyes. The way he's staring at me is like an apex predator hungrily surveying his timid prey. And that's pretty damn close to reality, when I think about it. I am totally at Breaker's mercy, and I can't imagine anywhere else I would rather be right now. Once I've neatly folded all my clothes and draped them in a pink velvet armchair in the corner of my bedroom, Breaker snaps his fingers to call me over again. I stand before him, goosebumps popping up on my bare skin in the cool air. He reaches out and lays his hands on my hips, pulling me closer. With a possessive snarl, he leans in and kisses my taut stomach, making me sharply inhale. His hands slide around to grope my ass, clearly enjoying how plush and soft my bum is. I have never put much thought into how I look, not in the past six years anyway. In fact, the fear of being hunted down by the motorcycle club urged me to try and make myself as unobtrusive as possible. To blend in and hide in the crowd. But Breaker doesn't see me that way. He makes me feel truly exceptional and desirable. I am worth fighting for. Worth killing for.

Nothing is as liberating and exhilarating as that knowledge.

This is a man who has killed for me once and would do so again in a heartbeat. And if he wants me —all of me, whatever I have to offer—then he is more than welcome to take what belongs to him.

"I'm going to fill your sweet little pussy up," he whispers roughly. "I'm going to pound you senseless. I'm going to fuck you bare and let you feel every inch of my cock. Is that what you want, Kate? You want me to fuck your tight little hole?"

I feel nearly dizzy with want. Nobody has ever said words like this to me. It's more addicting than any drug. It's more thrilling than any freefall. It's everything I want and everything I never knew I needed. I can hardly contain my desire. I can so clearly recall the moment I dropped his name to Caitlyn in the breakroom at work. The way those two syllables fell from my lips and hung in the air. I knew I was flirting with danger when I dared to breathe his name, though I had no idea how much. I still don't understand how he found out about it. Has he been watching me somehow? Has Breaker been stalking me, keeping an eye on my movements and choices from a safe distance? Has he been here all along, those dark eyes riveted to my body as I walk from my car to the massage parlor? Has he followed me home across town to my apartment? Has he watched me take the stairs up to my place, seen me undressing through the window in the evening? Has he been so close he could smell me, and yet I didn't even know?

After all, he clearly knew where I live, where I work. He knew that I live by myself, and he knew what time I would be home. Has he kept an elaborate account of my life for the past six years, diligently tailing me from place to place around town?

The very idea is thrilling. Imagining those dark, hawk like eyes following me as I innocently went throughout my day as usual. I wonder what he was thinking about me all those times. I wonder if there were any close calls. Did he stay perfectly hidden all the time, or did he push the limits? Did he play a game of getting as close to me as possible without my noticing? I can imagine him trailing me through the local mall, standing nearby when I go into dressing rooms. Did he picture me taking off my clothes and standing naked in front of the mirror? Did he dream about one day breaking through that impossible barrier and just nabbing me in public, taking me back under his wing because he just can't resist me?

Is he obsessed with me? Does this go far beyond our established roles of protector and protected? Somewhere along the way, did his feelings toward me change from fatherly defender to sensual suitor? I wonder how long he has been holding back. How long has he been aching for me? Have there been any other girls, or has he been waiting to steal me back all this time?

I can feel myself getting wetter just thinking about that.

I have never wanted anyone or anything as badly as I want Breaker. I should have known one day it would come to this. For six years, I have lived with a chip on my shoulder, constantly looking around for signs of danger. I should have predicted that Breaker would not let me go so easily. He's my savior, my king. He's been the silent center and focus of my universe ever since we first met even though I never allowed myself to accept it. And now that he's here again, in front of me, I don't want to be away from him ever again. I want to be as close as humanly possible, feel his hard, glorious body sliding and rutting against mine. I want to feel him inside me, filling me and making me feel whole again. I had no idea how desperately I need this, but there's no going back now. I am his, and I cannot wait for him to claim me for real.

"Get on the bed," Breaker orders, and I do as I'm told.

I climb onto the bed and lie there on my back, waiting for his next lesson. I watch, holding my breath tight in my throat, as Breaker slowly strips off his clothes, never breaking eye contact with me. I can feel my body warming up and my mouth starts to water as more and more of his amazing, powerful body is revealed. Those rippling hard abs. His broad, strong back. His bulging biceps. Those thick legs that could dash and vault with ease. He's like a god on earth, and I can't wait to be converted.

Silently, Breaker walks over and grabs both my wrists, fastening them to the wooden headboard post with a loose hair ribbon on my nightstand. I breathe heavily with anticipation, watching him climb onto the bed, looming over me. He leans down and kisses me softly, slipping one hand down between my legs. I gasp as he slides two thick fingers inside my virginal pussy, slowly working me open. The sensation is unlike anything I've ever experienced, even playing around by myself.

"Good girl," he growls. "Open yourself up for me."

"Yes, sir," I pant, feeling my pleasure mount higher and higher. I'm desperate for a release, but he stops before I can reach it. I whimper with disappointment, but Breaker smiles.

"Don't worry, kid. I've got something much better than that in store for you," he promises. He bends to kiss me, nibbling at my bottom lip as he positions himself between my thighs. I gasp and moan against his lips when I feel the velvety smooth head of his hard cock pressing into my tight, clenching hole. He teases me for a moment, circling my opening until I'm writhing and shuddering with need.

"I'm going to fuck you, Kate. I've wanted this for so long," he whispers harshly against the shell of my ear. I shiver and groan with mingled delicious pain and pleasure as his thick shaft spears into me, pushing me open. I feel tears stinging in my eyes as I close around him. Breaker groans and shoves into me hard, shattering through my hymen again and again. He slides in even deeper as I cry out with bliss, the tip of his cock striking a sensitive spot far within myself. I wriggle and rock against him, helpless with my hands bound over my head.

"Very good. Fuck, you're so tight and wet for me, little girl," Breaker hisses. "Does it feel good, princess? Do you like having my cock inside you?"

"Yes," I answer breathlessly. "Oh god, yes."

"You deserve to be punished, don't you?" he whispers.

"Yes, please. Punish me. Put me in my place," I breathe.

Breaker reaches up and tangles a handful of my hair in his fist, gently wrenching my head to one side so he can dive in, kissing and nipping at my ticklish neck. I buck up to meet his thrusts, shaking and whimpering incoherently. The pleasure is so intense, it feels like there are fireworks exploding behind my eyelids as I shut my eyes tight, giving in to the waves of intense sensation. Breaker pulls my hair and grazes my neck with his teeth while his cock pounds into me harder and faster, picking up speed as he begins to relinquish his tightly-held control over his body and his needs.

"Tell me, Kate. Tell me who you belong to," he commands gruffly.

"I'm yours, Breaker. I've always been yours," I gasp.

His other hand slips down to massage my sensitive clit as he fucks me, and I feel like I might faint from the pleasure.

"Oh—oh god," I murmur, tossing my head from side to side.

"Yes. Yes, princess. Just like that. I want you to come for me, Kate. Gush that sweet honey all over my fingers and cock," he snarls.

"I'm so close. Oh, it feels so good," I sigh.

Breaker's cock spears into me harder and deeper, a tinge of pain adding another aspect of complex pleasure to the magical concoction of chemicals in my body. I hook my legs around his waist, pulling him in as his cock pounds my tight hole again and again, both of us ratcheting higher and higher until finally, Breaker's hand falls over my neck. He gently presses down, just enough to intensify how I feel, and at the precise same time, we come together. I shudder and moan, my pussy clenching around his hard cock as he spurts his hot, precious seed deep inside me. We move against one another, riding through the shockwaves of pleasure, slowly coming down from the most earth-shattering high I have ever experienced.

For a moment, Breaker rests his forehead against mine. All is quiet. He slowly withdraws from me, his seed and my come gushing out together. I lay here totally exhausted while he unties my wrists, kissing them gently where they've rubbed a little raw. He starts to get dressed and, as he's bringing me my little pile of clothes, I hear a familiar sound outside.

A motorcycle engine revving.

Breaker's eyes flit over to the window and a scowl passes over his face. He glances back to me and I ask, "What's going to happen now?"

"Do you hear that?" he says, dodging the question.

"The bikes? Yeah, I think it might just be the show on TV in the living," I offer.

He shakes his head. "No. I turned that off earlier. Get dressed. Now," he orders.

"Okay," I murmur, hurriedly following his command.

"The girl you mentioned my name to," he begins gruffly, "what is her name?"

"Caitlyn. Why?" I ask, frowning.

"Shit. Tell me more," he says, glancing at the window. The bikes are getting louder.

Closer.

"Caitlyn isn't anyone to worry about," I try to brush it off.

"Don't be so sure. The mole could be anywhere. What else do you know about this woman, Kate?" Breaker demands.

I wrack my brain as I pull on my clothing. "Um. I don't know. She works at the massage parlor with me. She's outgoing. Friendly. The clients love her."

"Go on," he urges.

I sigh and give him a shrug. "Breaker, I don't know her very well."

"Yes, but I bet she knows all about you," he says grimly.

"We don't talk very much," I insist. "Although…"

Oh no. A memory resurfaces in my mind, something I never thought twice about until now. I look at Breaker with horror.

"Oh god. There was a conversation we had a while back in December. She was complaining to me about how she was angry that her boyfriend couldn't give her a ride back to her parents' place for Christmas because… because… he only drives a motorcycle," I murmur.

"There it is," Breaker points out.

"Shit. How could I have been so stupid?" I whimper, holding my face in my hands.

Breaker grabs his leather jacket and pulls it on, then offers me a hand. He pulls me to my feet, and as he heads toward the door, I glance out the window. My heart nearly drops to my stomach when my eyes behold the sight outside.

At least a dozen motorcycles and their riders assembled in the parking lot. All looking toward my window. Toward me.

"Kate, get down!" Breaker shouts at me, just as the sound of gunfire rings out, matching the rumble of thunder breaking overhead.

I lunge forward and wrap my arms around Kate, tackling her to the ground with as much care as I can put into the snap reaction just before bullets spray across the outside of the apartment. I feel pieces of drywall pattering against my back, and window glass shatters all around us, followed by water from the rain pouring outside. Kate's body is shaking, but she holds a hand over her mouth to stop herself from screaming.

She starts to move as soon as we're on the ground, but I hold her tight to me as a storm of bullets starts spraying again and peppers the opposite wall. It knocks a painting off, and a stray bullet ricochets and hits the bedside lamp. Kate flinches in terror, but I shush her, not letting her out of my arms.

"Not yet," I snarl as adrenaline starts to course

through my body, heightening my senses and making time itself feel different. "Don't move!"

"Who's out there?!" she cries, keeping her head down against my chest.

"I have a guess," I growl.

I have to make a plan, and I have to make one fast. I can hear screams coming from the rest of the building. I know damn well the only people who could be out there are Buzz's club, maybe even the man himself. The longer we're here, the more innocent people who are about to get dragged into things. And the longer we're in this room, the more likely it is Kate is going to get hurt.

That's not happening on my watch.

I've watched over Kate for so long, gotten to know every step of her life. I've desired her. A big part of me has been waiting for what happened today, hungering for it with a power that kept me watching her every move with such unfailing dedication. Now that she's in my grasp, I'm not going to let her come to harm—least of all by the likes of Buzz and the gang of glory-hungry dipshits he calls a club.

I'd sooner die than let that happen.

Lucky for us, I've been ready for this day for a long time without even meaning to be. In all the preparations I've made to stay in touch with whatever Kate's doing, I've learned the layout of her apartment complex better than her own superintendent. I've walked the very halls outside before. I've even stolen CCTV footage and gotten to know which routes people use most and which areas are quietest.

But that doesn't make me bulletproof. If I want to pull this off, I can't just be prepared. I have to be quick, decisive, and make the right decision every time.

I have to pull this off perfectly, and anything short of that is going to get us both killed.

As soon as the gunfire stops, I get up just enough to lunge for the bed. I grab the mattress with both hands, and the surge of adrenaline I get at the thought of Kate being at risk here gives me strength to rip the entire thing from the bed frame as if it were made of Styrofoam. Kate lets out a gasp as I swing it over her head and thrust it against the bedroom window to create a makeshift barrier.

It won't last long, but it'll keep the pouring rain out, and with a little luck, it might just buy us some time to make it out of here.

No sooner have I put the mattress up than I hear bullets start to hit it, and my eyes dart around the room. Her closet is open, and I see something in it that catches my attention. Kate starts to stand up, but I hold a hand out to her as I cross the room to the closet.

"Not yet!" I bark, and she crawls closer to the bed frame, eyes wide and face pale.

"What the hell are you doing?!" she shouts as I grab a hard-shelled suitcase from the closet and hold it up. "We don't have time to pack, we need to get out of here!"

"I'm not packing!" I bark, kneeling down and putting my hands at the hinges. I grit my teeth and pull as hard as I can, and with a ripping and cracking sound, the suitcase tears apart in my hands at the zipper. "I'm giving us a shield!"

I hurry back over to Kate and grab my jacket from the floor nearby. Without waiting for her to react, I throw it over her shoulders and guide one of her arms into a sleeve. She catches onto what I'm doing and takes over putting my jacket on while I click the straps inside the bigger half of the suitcase together, giving her a little body armor.

"It won't stop a bullet, but it's all we've got right now, and it might just deflect a little debris," I say, using the smaller half of the suitcase to make a makeshift shield for myself. "Kate, we've got to move fast and not hesitate, not for anything, do you understand me?"

"Yes!" she shouts, and without another second wasted, I grab her hand and run.

I feel something ding the edge of my 'shield' hard as we exit the room, but I'm not stopping for anything. We race down the hallway, keeping low, and I stop at the living room to check the window before darting out.

"Oh god," Kate gasps, clapping a hand over her mouth.

The living room windows are shot out too, and broken glass litters the couch and floor. Some of the bullets made it into the kitchen, and splintering bullet holes have splashed across the wooden cabinets. A microwave with two holes in the door sparks feebly.

"They think we're still in the bedroom, go!" I shout after realizing they aren't actively firing into the living room right now. Still clutching Kate's hand, I lead her through her own apartment and throw the front door open. I hear the sound of jingling keys behind me, and I barely register it as we rush out into the hallway.

The gunfire hasn't gone unnoticed.

Tenants are already staggering out of their apartments. A middle-aged man is hugging two crying children to him across the hall, three elderly women are helping each other get down on the ground in the hallway and cover their heads, and a young couple are fumbling with their phones, presumably to call the police.

"Everyone!" I bark as I lead Kate through the hallway and toward the stairs, "stay on the floor, get in the hallways and stay on the floor! If you can't leave your homes, get in the bathtub and stay down!"

My clear, authoritative voice gets people's attention, and the ones who are still poking their heads out of their apartment doors start to obey, one by one.

"Anyone calling 911," I shout, "ask for Officer Dan McArthur! Daniel McArthur," I repeat, making eye contact with anyone holding a phone as I guide Kate along. "He'll get you to safety! Stay away from the windows and do *not* go outside!"

I don't wait for anyone to reply. We don't have time for that. I'm not these people's hero, anyway. I'm the villain come to collect what's mine and get out, and that's what I'm going to do.

"Who's that cop you named?" Kate says as I throw the door to the stairs open and check it to make sure it's empty. There's nobody in sight, and I don't hear the sounds of running booted feet, so I tug Kate along and start running down the stairs as fast as I can without getting us killed.

"Dan's on the take," I explain hurriedly. "I've got cops in half the state."

"Why do you need someone in Cheyenne?!" she asks, incredulous.

"Think I'm giving away all my secrets that easy?" I ask, casting a wink back at her.

We rush down the stairs until we come to the ground floor, where I hear the sounds of shouts that don't sound as panicked as they ought to. My gut senses are sending up red flags, and instead of rushing past it like I planned, I hold a finger to my lips at Kate and lead her against the wall.

Sure enough, the voice getting closer becomes clearer by the second.

"You sweep the halls, I'll check the stairs!" a gruff young man's voice comes muffled through the door just before he pushes it open.

I don't see a man step through those doors. I see a male body wearing Buzz's kutte, and that's all I need to see. Without warning, hesitation, or so much as a breath, my body lurches forward with a raised fist. The punk has a second to turn his face and see the whites of my eyes when it's far too late to do anything about it.

My fist collides with his nose, and I feel bones crunch as his face crumples. The man drops like a rock, and I let the door close behind him just before he hits the ground, out cold.

"Holy shit, holy shit," Kate gasps, nearly hyper-ventilating before I grab her hand again and keep moving.

I take her down the next floor to the basement, where there are already a couple of people taking cover that give us petrified, sheet-white looks before cowering away. I'm glad none of them are armed—I look like exactly the kind of guy who's responsible for the shooting here.

"Stay low and stay quiet," I hiss in the basement as I lead Kate across it to my destination: an old shelf that conceals an emergency exit the kids in the apartment like to use. I've seen them run down here dozens of times, and on the stolen CCTV cameras, I saw them reappear in the garage. Normally, the only garage access is outside. It's a long shot, but it's our only chance.

"Where is this going to take us?" Kate asks as I shove the shelf aside to reveal the doorway.

"Garage," I say. "You saw me park my bike by the building across the street, so we're going to need to make a run for it. Keep that suitcase up and don't let go."

"Wait!" she says, and I hear that jingling again as she fumbles with her pocket.

She takes out a ring of keys, and she tosses them to me. I catch them in one hand, furrowing my brow.

"Take my car," she says, "it's on the first floor of the garage, and it'll give us a way out with more protection than a suitcase."

I flash her a grin and nod.

"Ever tell you I'm glad I saved you?" I say as I lead her through the exit as the other tenants look on, stunned.

We race out to the parking garage, which is empty, as far as I can tell. It's empty insofar as there aren't any gunmen in eyesight right now, which is better than I was expecting, frankly.

I see her car immediately, and I don't have time to wait any longer. I pick Kate up and run with her before she can so much as finish giving a yelp of protest.

"That's my car, right there!" she says hurriedly.

"I know," I snap.

"Shit, right," she says as I come skidding to a halt by the trunk. Before I can set her down, she has hopped out of my arms and made it halfway to the passenger side door. I hop into the driver's seat, and as soon as she shuts her door, I peel out of the parking space and screech out of the parking garage.

My heart skips a beat at what I see as soon as I do.

Buzz brought an army with him. There must be nearly a dozen bikes out front, some of which have their rider on them, but most empty. The apartment must be crawling with men by now. All the better that I'm getting us out of here. The sooner they realize what they're looking for isn't there, the sooner they'll leave those innocent people alone and come after us.

If only that last part weren't so tricky.

I see someone's head turn in our direction, and the rider shouts to the other. Time's up. I turn the wheels in the opposite direction and gun it, and the screeching of tires announces our departure while the sound of roaring engines behind me tells me we aren't going to make the stealthy getaway I was hoping for.

I'm barely halfway down the block before I see motorcycles in the rear-view mirror.

"Get down!" I shout, using the handbrake to careen around a corner and try to shake them. Kate's car isn't built for speed, but in a city, I just need to put as much between us as I possibly can. If they're chasing me and trying to follow Buzz's orders, they won't be careful, and that means we might just stand a chance.

But before I clear the corner, we feel something hit the car toward the back, followed by the unmistakable sound of a tire bursting, and the car starts spinning.

We've been hit, and this car isn't getting far with a blown-out tire.

I guide the spinning car as it careens through the narrow street and comes to an abrupt halt several yards down it. By the time we stop, Kate is clutching the dashboard and looking terrified, but her attention snaps to the rear-view mirror at the same time as mine does. We ended up facing the same direction we were headed, but with a tire blown out, there's no chance in hell we're about to outrun these guys.

"Shit!" she shouts, "Can we still drive on this?"

"Yeah, but not in a way that's gonna let us shake these fucks," I say, throwing the car into reverse. "Hold on."

"What?!" she blurts, snatching the seatbelt and scrambling to fasten it.

I stomp down on the gas, and the car flies backward toward the intersection.

Kate clutches the dashboard and lets out a steady stream of curses under her breath as I keep my attention on throwing the car back in as straight a line as possible while building speed. What I'm doing is beyond risky, but it's less risky than trying to outrun a pack of Buzz's men on a blown-out tire.

Just as we hit the corner, so do the bikers.

I hear shouts, curses, gunshots, and the sounds of a lot of tires screeching as the pack swerves to avoid the car I just reversed into their stream of oncoming traffic. Most of them manage to swerve out of the way, but one lays his bike down and skids, spinning and clipping the back of the car and rolling off limply.

"Get out and stay behind the car, we're going for *that* bike," I shout, and I don't have time for her to respond before I get out of the car and dart for the laid-down bike. The rider has just started to push himself up, and as soon as he sees me, he reaches for the gun at his side.

I reach him first. Barely stopping, I stoop down to one knee and bring my fist down on his face, hard, and it cracks his head against the asphalt, putting him out cold. Before I can even make sure he's out, I reach for that gun he was going for and take it from him, aiming it ahead of me and firing as soon as I see bikes.

One of my shots ricochets off the metal of someone's bike, and another hits a man in the arm.

The gang takes the next block's corner to get away from my suppressing fire, and I know our window of opportunity is rapidly shrinking. We have enough time to get on this bike and get out, and I can only hope the accident didn't damage the vehicle too badly. Kate comes running as soon as she sees me propping the bike up, and she has hopped on the back of it before I can even get fully seated.

"Is he dead?" Kate breathes, clutching me from behind and looking down at the man whose bike I'm stealing.

"No, and he'll be thanking me if his buddies don't get off our ass," I grunt, and I peel away from the site of the accident, heading in the very direction we came from. It's not ideal, but heading down the road we spun or continuing onward just sets us up for the pack to intercept us. Back is the only way they won't be expecting.

I don't know the streets of Cheyenne as well as I'd like, I'm riding a bike that isn't my own, and there's a gang whose tactics are as unpredictable as their leader chasing us. I can swear I feel Kate's racing heartbeat on my back, and I can't blame her. The sounds of engines aren't that far behind us, and no matter how many turns I take through alleys and narrow side-streets, they're always just a few steps behind us. And if we take things onto the highway, the police will be on us in no time. Our cop on the take is useful, but I don't have the kind of resources to keep *this* level of heat off us.

Another turn takes us down a street with several hotel garage parking complexes on it, and I move us into the second one down, guiding us behind a concrete pillar and waiting in the shadows to see if I've managed to buy us a breather. Kate's hands are cold around me, and I reach down to warm them as we watch the stream of bikes roll past the block from the outside. They're moving slower than the last time I saw them, and I can't help but think there are fewer of them now than it sounded like.

Something's up, but I can't tell what exactly, not yet.

"How the hell did they get here this fast?" I murmur.

"They knew you were coming to find me?" she asks.

"They shouldn't have," I growl. "In the inside left pocket of my jacket, there's a cloth, can you hand it to me?"

She pauses, then obliges me, and I run the rag over my face and shake it out while we have a breather.

"It's about as far from their clubhouse to here as it is from mine to here," I say.

"Wait, yours?" she asks, and it occurs to me that we've barely had time to catch up.

"A lot has changed, kid," I say, glancing back at

her with a tired smile. "Didn't think I could keep an eye on you while flying solo, did you?"

"I didn't know what to expect, honestly," she says, and I have to wonder... just how much was *she* thinking about me in the time we've been apart?

"I run a club not far from Devil's Tower," I explain, deciding to tell her before I second guess myself. "Turns out, I wasn't the only one who wanted to split from Buzz as soon as everything went down with you. He never backed down on his new 'business model'. He's been recruiting groupies while the core members split off and joined me. Nobody's turned a gun on me yet, so I figure I'm doing an alright job," I say, still watching the roads outside through the openings in the parking garage between floors.

She's quiet for a moment before saying, "I'm surprised to hear you tell me all that."

"Me too," I admit, looking back at her. "But if we're going to get through this together, we've got to trust each other. You did a hell of a lot more to trust me back there than I'd ever expect, so you earned a little truth."

"I... thanks," she says after a moment's hesitation. "But what happens now?"

"Now, we figure out how to get you out of here safely," I say, leaning on the handles of the bike. "I found you because I bugged your phone. Sorry, by the way, but apparently, it was for your own good."

She tenses, but after a disapproving murmur, she says nothing more.

"So, the only ways Buzz could know I was coming down here for you is one of two things: either he *also* bugged your phone, which isn't likely, or he got tipped off right around the same time I found out you were talking about me. And there's only one person I know you were giving my name to," I add as her eyes go wide.

"Caitlyn," she breathes.

"I need to know *everything*, Kate," I say, turning around and knitting my brow at her. "You've got more than enough evidence to put me behind bars for life if you want, so this is all to help you. Anything you tell me makes it that much more likely we get out of here without a few extra pounds of bullets in us."

"I don't know anything else!" Kate says, exasperated. "I told you her boyfriend rides, but he doesn't… I mean… don't take this the wrong way, but he doesn't *look* like a biker, not like you and the other guys do," she says, holding up my kutte she's still wearing.

I glare into her eyes, searching for anything that she could be holding back, but she glares right back, and I have to chuckle after a moment, shaking my head.

"Wait," she says, and I quirk an eyebrow. "She works at a massage parlor, and her boyfriend rides a bike but doesn't look like a biker. Groupies are like that guy Moxie was with when you dropped me off in Stonedale, right?" she asks, sounding more alarmed by the moment. I nod, and she continues, but I think I see where she's going with this, and I don't like it. "What if… you don't think Caitlyn is someone Buzz has already gotten to, do you?"

"I've been suspecting for a while that Buzz is going broader than I thought," I say, stroking my chin. "I didn't have proof yet, but it adds up: that boyfriend of Caitlyn's might be one of Buzz's groupies who hasn't earned his patches. He'd be dying for a piece of intel like this to pass along to his boss. Caitlyn would be an easy accomplice, willing or not."

"Goddamnit," she breathes.

"It's part of why I never rounded up my men and tried to take out Buzz for good," I admit, running a hand over my face and clenching my jaw momentarily. "He's not running a club, he's running a gang of reckless young men he has doing his dirty work when he realized pimping wasn't going to be that easy."

There's nothing dishonest about my words. I don't want the blood of that many aimless kids on my hands, because if I brought my club to war against Buzz, there would be a lot of blood between me and him.

"Alright," I say, lifting my head and revving the

engine. "Here's the plan. I have one more solid contact in Cheyenne I've been saving for a rainy day: someone who works at the impound lot. We can't take this bike any further out of the city, it'll draw way too much attention, assuming it doesn't break down on us. We get a new ride there and head back up to my place up north. We can regroup from there, and you'll have a safe place to hide."

"If that's our only option, I'm game," she says, taking a deep breath.

I text my contact, and it's only a minute before he gets back to me to confirm that he'll be ready. I carefully pull out of the parking garage and head toward the outskirts of town, keeping a careful eye on the roads. Avoiding police is easy enough, but I'm surprised to see just how empty the roads are of bikers. I can't imagine they packed up and left that quickly, and it's all the more reason for us to hurry.

Ten minutes later, I'm slowing the bike down at the chain link gates of the impound park. It's a large and industrial place with no decor and very little indication as to what it even is, besides the rows upon rows of cars in different states of disrepair.

I pull the bike just inside the gates, then bring it to a slow stop and get off with Kate and gesture for her to follow me. I check my phone, and I see the latest message from my contact.

"He has a car picked out for us," I say, closing the phone and pocketing it. "It's just over here. Says it's a black sedan, so it'll feel just like old times," I add, flashing a grin at Kate as she walks close to me.

"Don't fix it if it isn't broke, I guess," she says, looking around warily. "Are you sure about this guy of yours, Breaker? Something feels… too easy about this."

I open my mouth to put her at ease, but now that she mentions it, I have to admit, I've been unsure whether the strange feeling in my gut is just nerves or something more. I slow to a stop, giving her a thoughtful look, then nodding.

"No, you're right," I say, taking my phone back out. "Let me call my guy and see if he'll meet us over here."

I call the number and listen to the rings, but after just three, the line goes dead.

And that's when I hear the whistle. It comes from behind us, and we turn around to a heart-stopping sight.

It's Buzz.

Gray haired and grizzled as a bear, aged faster than he should have after the loss of his son, the man who I used to look up to like a father stands at the end of the alley of cars we're standing in, gun trained on me, and there are men on either side of him, all armed and ready for a show. The wind blows his tattered kutte gently, but he looks as still as a statue as he considers pulling the trigger on me. The sounds of more footsteps behind us tells me we're surrounded.

This was a trap.

"Now that I've got your attention," Buzz says in a slow, hate-filled voice that's dripping with bloodlust, "maybe we can finally have that conversation. Man to man. No guns, no tricks."

To my surprise, Buzz puts his weapons down, and the rest of the men in the gang around us follow suit, even going so far as to take their ammo out of their guns. Buzz has some honor left, at least. As tempting as it is to just blow his brains out right here and now, I give the faintest of nods, take the clip out of my pistol, and toss it aside too.

"What are you doing?" Kate hisses.

"We're outgunned," I murmur quietly. "If I don't give mine up, they'll pick theirs back up faster than I can kill 'em all."

Kate nods softly, and I take a few steps forward to match Buzz's. We're still a distance apart, but the crowd is gathering in a loose circle around us, and I can tell Buzz has them under orders for this. He doesn't just want revenge. He wants to make an example of me.

"Found out about your friend here at the lot," Buzz says casually, holding up a phone and waving it in the air before tossing it aside carelessly. "Gotta say, you learned well, Breaker. You would have made a good enforcer one day."

"You would have shown your real colors eventually," I say, staring him down. I can still hear Kate shifting behind me, and most of my thoughts are on her. I have to keep her safe, no matter what, first and foremost. I'm an honorable man, but I'm not above sucker-punching Buzz and grabbing Kate to get out of here if it means keeping her out of harm's way. "If you think I would have ridden with you much longer, you're stupider than I thought."

An agitated jeer goes through the crowd, but Buzz just chuckles.

"When you talk to me like that, boy, you make me regret the day I took you in. You were like kin to me, you know that?" he says, not hiding the furious edge in his voice.

"So were you," I say, "until I found out what you're really like. You'd throw a woman's life away even faster than these kids you've suckered into your flimsy little empire," I add, gesturing around at the onlookers.

"Enough," Buzz snarls. "I don't want to hear that kind of talk from you, of all people. Not over Roadster's grave." He cracks his knuckles and starts approaching me, and every muscle in my body is poised. "That's why I stopped you here. So you can answer for your crimes. I want you to know exactly how Roadster felt when you murdered him."

He reaches into his pocket, and for a moment, I think he's about to pull a gun on me, but instead, he takes out a shining pair of brass knuckles that he slips over his meaty fingers. My jaw tenses, and I look back at Kate meaningfully.

She's already a step ahead of me, reaching into my pockets and taking out mine. She looks at them uneasily for a moment, then nods to me and tosses them over. I catch them and slip them on, watching Buzz's gaze carefully.

"Those are the same ones, aren't they?" Buzz growls. "You're a real son of a bitch, you know that, Breaker?"

"How much have you been playing up how much you loved Roadster, Buzz?" I ask, as much to the crowd as to Buzz, whose face goes red. "That kid idolized you, and you gave him shit at every turn. Nothing ever good enough. Roadster died because he was more loyal to you than you were to him."

"I gave you both better than you ever deserved, you cock-sucking pussy," he says, advancing on me.

"My mom gave me better than I deserved," I say, readying myself. "All *you* ever gave me was a push out the door."

Buzz charges, the groupies roar in approval, and I throw a punch to receive him... just before his fist connects with my jaw.

Everything is simultaneously blurred and crystal clear. I feel as though I could be standing in the background of a famous impressionist painting, the colors all stretched and watery from the pouring rain. All around me, there was a dense wall of loud noise and frantic activity as the dozen or so members of the motorcycle club rushed to close me off from the one man I could count on to keep me safe from them. Tears sting in my eyes and burn hot tracks down my cheeks, mingling with the pelting shoots of rain. A thick fog is settling in around us, like being sucked into a massive cloud, obscuring and disfiguring the world, only adding to the sense of panic and doom hovering over the crowd.

I don't know what to do. I don't know where to go. On all sides, the big, burly MC members are closing in on me. I can see their rough faces scowling and glaring at me with combined hatred and interest. It's the latter that makes me more nervous, to be honest. There's a large part of my psyche that has never fully moved on from the trauma of being locked up in that room six years ago, at the mercy of scary strange men who could easily bend and break me to their satisfaction. Over the years, I've had countless nightmares in which I find myself back in that godforsaken stale-smelling bedroom, my fists bruising and collecting tiny, painful splinters as I frantically and helplessly bang them on the locked door. I have woken up in the middle of the night, shrieking and paralyzed with terror, thinking that I am still stuck in that room waiting for my inevitable dark fate to come along and destroy me once and for all. I've played through those foggy, fearful memories a thousand times, asking myself to figure out another way out that didn't rely on Breaker having to commit murder to save me. But I always come back to the same conclusion: that there was no other way, that Breaker did what he had to do to save me and if he hadn't, I would still be there today. Or, God forbid, somewhere worse.

And now, standing trapped in this crowd of angry, strong man, I feel just as helpless and lost and small as I did that night six years ago. I feel someone grab my arm, thick sausage fingers wrapping around my wrist and pulling me tight. I let out a bloodcurdling scream of horror and try my hardest to wrench away from the man gripping me, but he is just too strong and I am too small to fight back. I have always thought of myself as a fairly self-possessed young woman in control of my fate, at least to some degree. But there's nothing like being reminded of how weak and fragile you are physically to make you feel weak and fragile mentally.

The man who grabbed me leans in close to my face. I can feel the roughness of his stubble scratching against my own softer skin. His breath is hot and sour as he hisses a threat against the shell of my ear. I shudder and try to pull away but he is too powerful for me to fight back, no matter how hard I try.

"You slippery, conniving little bitch," he snarls in my ear. "I bet you thought you were going to actually escape our grasp, huh? Sorry, little girl: you can run but you can't hide from Buzz's gang."

"I don't understand," I whimper helplessly. "What do you want from me? I'm just a regular girl! I don't have money, I don't have anything!"

The man sneers at me, the flames of red-hot rage and lust crackling in his sharp gaze. "You have no idea how much you've cost us, Katie. But nobody gets out of paying what's due. Nobody. And we're here now to make you pay. If you can't pay with coin then it'll have to be flesh and blood," he hisses cruelly.

I stick my chin out defiantly and retort, "It's not Katie. It's Kate, you moron!"

The color drains from his face as it dawns on him that I just insulted him outright. He tightens his grip around my wrist and wrenches my arm behind my back, yanking me against his chest. A flash of sharp pain shoots through my arm and I feel dizzy, almost going limp.

"You'll learn your place soon enough," he snaps. "Especially once Buzz snuffs out your Prince Charming over there!"

"Don't hurt him!" I scream as tears and rainwater pelt into my open mouth.

I swallow hard and try to jump up to see what's happening beyond the crowd of big, sweaty, disgusting men around me. I know Breaker is surrounded by enemies—and the worst kind of enemy at that: former friends. Hell hath no fury like a friend turned against you.

"The both of you are going to finally get what you deserve," the man holding me snarls.

"Leave him alone!" I screech.

I try my hardest to twist around and kick my assailant in the shins, but he's got too firm a grasp on me. "Nice try, kiddo, but you can't take Diesel down that easy," he guffaws.

I manage to crane my neck to one side to stare

around the thick body of another club member in front of me to see the man called Buzz grappling with an enraged Breaker. My heart drops into my stomach as I watch with horror. Breaker is impossibly quick and strong. I know that without any hesitation. But Buzz seems to be a decent match for him, maybe even just because of his decades of experience. Both men have their sleeves rolled up to their elbows, their massive hands curled into tight, angry fists. Buzz wears an unsettling sneer on his heavy, intimidating features, but when Breaker's eyes flit over to the crowd for a moment, his gaze automatically locks with mine. I see the realization dawning on his handsome, rugged face that I'm being held against my will by the man called Diesel, presumably yet another former friend-turned-enemy of Breaker's. His face drains of color at the sight of Diesel's meaty hands controlling me, and then he lets out a terrifying battle cry and lunges at Buzz.

"Breaker!" I wail, tears and rain slicking my hair down to the sides of my face as I watch the man I adore trade crushing blows with his opponent.

Both of them are so fueled by rage and hatred and betrayal, and anyone can plainly see that this is a battle forged long ago, six years in the making. They have both itched for this moment for a long time, the opportunity to finally set the record straight. The two of them can't share the same planet anymore. There's not enough space in the universe for these men to coexist. It's a battle to the death, and they're so fairly matched who can tell which one will win?

My money is on Breaker, but my heart pangs with fear for him just the same.

Diesel's hands rove down my squirming body, violating me in a way I have not experienced since that fateful event six years ago. At first, I just freeze up with shock, but then my fighting instinct kicks in. Self-righteous anger mingles with the adrenaline pumping through my veins and I manage to swivel around and spit directly in Diesel's sneering face. He's so stunned and disgusted by my little attack that he lets go of me for half a second. I don't hesitate to break away from him and start bolting away, hoping to get closer to Breaker. I doubt there's much I can offer to help him now that he's up against his former boss and father figure in a battle of strength, but I'll be damned if I let my mysterious prince face this all alone. He's surrounded by enemies who all want him dead, and I need him to know I'm here, adoring and supporting him through the horror-show unfolding. But before I can make it out of the crowd and into the relatively clear little arena between Breaker and Buzz, another set of powerful, thickly-muscled arms grab hold of me and yank me back.

"Oh no, you don't," quips my assailant.

"Get your filthy hands off of me!" I screech.

My arms flail out as I dig in my heels, screaming incoherently, my own anger propelling me forward. Still, the man is stronger. He pulls me back and grasps my wrists pinned behind my back. At least now I have a better vantage point of the battle, though I start to regret getting a front row seat when Buzz's fist connects sharply with Breaker's jaw and I hear a dizzying crunch. The men all hiss and moan, excitedly watching their leader punish Breaker.

I cry out with fear for my handsome savior, but to my relief he manages to recover from the blow fairly quickly. He swipes a hand over his painful jaw, wincing a little before he bolts back toward Buzz. He rears his arm back and then pummels it forward, landing a sick blow to the Prez's gut. Buzz chokes out a gasp and doubles over, his arms wrapped around his midsection. Breaker seizes this opportunity to jump the Prez, knocking him flat on his back and straddling the older man's body before he even has a chance to react. Breaker throws punch after punch to Buzz's face, pinning the man down so that he can't fight back. I feel a powerful surge of hope light up within my chest and I watch with wide eyes as sprays of scarlet blood shoot through the air. I can only assume Breaker has shattered the older man's nose by the looks of it.

Then a body comes shooting past me through the crowd, stumbling out into the arena to grab a fistful of fabric at the back of Breaker's shirt. He yanks him back off of Buzz and to his feet, and I realize a moment later it was Diesel who cut in. Before Breaker can fully round on Diesel, Buzz wobbles to his own feet, one hand clapped over his bloody nose.

"Get back, Diesel! This doesn't involve you!" Buzz shouts hoarsely.

"But Buzz—" he tries to protest.

Buzz holds up his free hand to silence him, glaring at the younger recruit with warning.

"Get out of the way. This is between Breaker and me. Only one of us can finish this," he hisses, then turns to Breaker with a devilish glare. "I dare you, Breaker. End this. Do your worst. I can take it, you traitorous bastard!"

I look over fearfully at Breaker, but to my surprise, he shakes his head. Dragging an arm across his bloody face, he shouts back, "Don't make me go there, Buzz. I've already taken everything from you I could possibly want. I'm done with you, okay? It's over."

"Like hell it's over! What are you, a pussy?" Buzz sneers back, even as blood dribbles down from his nose and mouth, as well as from a gash along his left temple. He looks terrible, but the man is dead-set on taking this battle to the end.

Breaker angrily spits at Buzz, his saliva tainted pink with blood that makes my heart skip a beat with worry. "Call off the goon squad, Buzz. I'm done fighting with you!" he snaps.

"No! It's not over until one of us is dead," Buzz insists, getting back into a fighting stance with both fists up. "Come on, kid. Show me what you've got. Show me the version of Breaker who slaughtered my son."

"That was an accident. A necessary evil," Breaker growls, narrowing his eyes.

"And I was never prouder of you, boy," Buzz cackles evilly. "Proudest moment of my life—you finally manning up and killing Roadster in cold blood."

"You're sick!" I wail at him, but Buzz doesn't even flinch or look my way.

He's laser-focused on Breaker, waiting for his next move. And he gets that move mere milliseconds later, when Breaker comes flailing at him, swinging punches left and right. With every crushing blow, another spray of sickly blood reddens the air and mingles with the slick rainwater gathering on the ground. In fact, the ground is so wet with water and blood that the two men are sliding around a little, struggling to find a solid foothold. Breaker jumps back a step and I can tell he's doing everything in his power to restrain his anger, but Buzz is more than willing to poke the bear.

"Come on, you cowardly bastard! Fight me like a man! Stand up to me!" he eggs Breaker on. Breaker snarls and lunges for the Prez once more. He grabs hold of his shirt collar and shakes him violently, then slams his forehead into Buzz's head with a solid crunch, and lets the Prez wobble and collapse to the ground in a dizzy, painful heap.

Breaker delivers one more violent kick to Buzz's ribs, causing the Prez to groan with agony, and then Breaker comes rushing over to me. The crowd, horrified and cowed by what they just watched, move out of his way. The man holding my arms releases me and steps back so that Breaker can pull me to him. He kisses the top of my head and I melt into his arms, reaching up to delicately touch my fingertips to his cuts and bruises.

"You're hurt," I murmur sorrowfully. "Breaker, we need to get out of here."

"I know. We will. I'll get you to safety now, I promise," he says emphatically.

Then I do a double take, my eyes locking onto something that is so horrific, so terrifying, that it takes a moment for it to click in my head that what I'm seeing is real. Buzz has gotten up from the ground and grabbed a nearby tire iron. He heaves it up in the air and starts silently rushing over to Breaker from behind, a devilish, desperate gleam in his eyes.

"Breaker!" I gasp, pointing over his shoulder at Buzz. "Watch out!"

Breaker's lightning-quick reflexes kick in and he swivels around just in time to catch the tire iron with both strong hands. By now, Buzz is visibly weakened, and it doesn't take much for Breaker to turn the iron back on the Prez and thrust it toward the older man. Hard. I shut my eyes just in time to hear a nauseating smash, then a heavy thump as Buzz's heavy body hits the ground. A roar of anger and sadness explodes from the collected crowd of bikers, telling me without a doubt that Buzz is dead. I open my eyes to see Breaker drop the tire iron and lift both arms over his head, glaring around at the horrified crowd. I can tell that none of these guys expected this outcome. They all came here under the strict impression that Buzz would win the battle, and now they're all disorganized and confused without their leader to focus on.

I rush over to Breaker's side and he puts an arm around me. Then he addresses the crowd, clearing his throat. "Listen up!" he begins in a loud, authoritative tone. "This cannot be the way things go. We cannot continue to pit brother against brother, brother against father, friend against ally. It's barbaric. It's pointless. And it does nothing to move any of us forward, you got it? Think of this as your official wake-up call. You have to change your ways. This life will always end in blood if you keep it up. If you want a way out, if you are dedicated to changing your life, you are more than welcome to join my own motorcycle club. We are a family and we take care of one another. Anyone who disobeys, anyone who dares lay a finger on any woman, child, or innocent will be swiftly dealt with. If you think you're up to the challenge of what I'm offering you right now, you will know where and how to find me. Learn from this, men. Learn and adapt."

And with that, he leads me back to the car with his arm around me, the early morning sun just beginning to cast its hopeful light over the world.

KATE

A month later, and it's as though every little piece of my shattered life has come apart. But it's not a bad thing. In fact, I'd say it's exactly the opposite. As it turned out, the half-life of fear and paranoia I was living for six years, always looking over my shoulder and waiting for the other shoe to drop, was not really a life worth continuing. Luckily, I don't have to make all these new changes by myself. I have Breaker right beside me, keeping me sane and reassuring me that all will be well. The two of us are so perfectly in sync these days, like we were never separated in the first place. Nowadays, I tend to think of those six horrible, long years as sort of the dead period, the void section of my life. I was so alone, so empty inside, and I never admitted to myself why that was. I assumed it was just the run-of-the-mill twenty-something ennui, but I know the truth now: I needed Breaker then just as desperately as I do now. He is my shining light, my rugged Prince Charming who I can always rely on to scoop me up and rescue me, regardless of the danger. After the shootout with Buzz and the rest of the former motorcycle gang, I ran away from my old life. I realize now that the only ally I ever had during that time, the one friend I thought I could trust, turned out to be the one woman I should have been most wary of. But now I'll never have to see Caitlyn again. I'll never have to face Diesel or Buzz or Roadster or any of those filthy slimebags Breaker used to run with. He's everything I need and everything I want, and every day spent together brings me new joy and excitement.

After what went down with Buzz and the gang, I was unsurprisingly brought in to be questioned by the local police. That makes perfect sense, considering that a death was involved. But luckily, I was interviewed by one of Breaker's friends on the take, a cop who was entirely sympathetic and patient with me as I explained to him in minute, bloody detail what happened that dark day. At first, he was a little wary, since he's still a cop at the end of the day. He has protocol to stick to, superior officers to report to. I could sense that he kept wondering how the hell he was going to explain all of this mess to his superiors in a way that would make coherent sense and also allow for Breaker and me to go free. But once I launched into a detailed explanation of how the gang seized and kidnapped me as a naive eighteen-year old years ago, how they held me captive and planned to sell me into a horrible life, he began to really get on-board with how things shook out. I convinced the cop to understand how truly heroic and good-hearted Breaker is, about how he came and rescued me when nobody else would or could. I revealed to the police officer that the gang were back for revenge on the fact that Breaker freed me and killed one of their own in the process, and that was pretty much all it took to convince him as to why Buzz's death was unavoidable. One of them was always going to die that day; I'm just beyond grateful and ecstatic that it wasn't Breaker. I can't imagine how gray and empty my life would be without him. The thought of it sends a shudder down my spine.

I never want to spend another day apart from him. Six years is long enough. Now, Breaker is mine forever. And I am his.

So, after the interview with the police was over, Breaker took me back to my torn-up shell of an apartment so I could hastily pack a bag. The two of us hightailed it out of town at top speed, anxious to leave Casper far behind us. After all, I have no real attachments to the place other than my boring job that barely paid my bills. What's there to lose? We decided to lie low for our own safety and sanity, and so we headed to Crook County to hide out for a while until the dust settled and cleared. Truth be told, I was already aching to get out of that town, and I wasn't too concerned about where we would end up, as long as Breaker stays by my side. Now that Buzz is dead and the gang have abandoned their years-long quest for revenge against me for escaping and defying them, there's no practical reason keeping me tethered to Breaker. I could cut out on my own and start over somewhere by myself, but I don't want to. I already lost him once. I sure as hell don't plan on letting him slip away again. Not if I have anything to do with it.

Right now, we're in a car riding through the scenic, rolling green plains of my home state, Wyoming. My eyes are wide, taking in every detail of the beautiful surroundings. It's wide and expansive, the land so flat that you can see for miles in every direction easily. It's an eerily pleasant feeling, being about to see so far. For once, it feels like I no longer have to look over my shoulder for the inevitable danger to sneak up on me. The world belongs to us now and we can take whatever piece of it we so desire.

I stare out the window, watching intently as we pass the occasional farmhouse or small homestead. We pass by an aesthetically-haunting old barn with peeling brick-red paint, the gigantic doors folding and collapsing in at the front with years of age, erosion, and decay. Maybe it's just the small-town

Wyoming girl in me, but I can't help but smile. That barn, even though it looks sad and lonely now, is a piece of history. Someone's great-great-great-grandfather probably built it and raised all sorts of farm animals and children alike there. It makes me wistful about the past and excited about the future at the same time. I wonder where Breaker and I will end up. I wonder if we will have a family. I'm sure we will. And the idea of carrying my handsome savior's child… god, I just can't wait.

As we drive through the pastoral countryside along the 113, Breaker points out places he has been, places he has helped to rebuild and restore over the years. Earlier, we passed by the famous Native American monument, the Devils Tower. It's a gorgeous, awe-inspiring rock formation that is integral to native culture and history. Breaker tells me all about how he has helped to protect it, defending the Tower against those who would seek to strip it of its power and significance in the name of imperialism and western expansion. He speaks of the Devils Tower so reverently and respectfully, like he truly understands how vital the monument is to preserving a part of history that is so constantly under threat. He also stood up to those who put the fate of the nearby towns in jeopardy, defending their honor when they were too small to fight it on their own. He even helped to rebuild several structures in the nearby inhabited areas, putting backbreaking labor into his pitch to keep these small, rural communities thriving and safe. It warms my heart to know that he has the kind of soul that leads him to fix other people's problems. Breaker is a complicated man. On the one hand, he won't hesitate to crack skulls together if the situation requires such action, but he also has a bit of 'world-saving' in him. He may be a hard man, but he's got a soft side, and I love that about him.

Hell, I love everything about him.

"Look, here's the place," Breaker says warmly, a rare smile on his rugged features.

My heart skips a beat as I sit up straight in the passenger seat, eyes wide. I look out the window to see that we are pulling up to the end of the road, where a glimmering, crystal-blue lake is gently lapping at the shore. Green plains grass billows romantically in the other direction as far as the eye can see. It's a truly scenic location, and perfect for the picnic we have planned.

"Oh, it's beautiful," I gasp excitedly.

Breaker pulls the car to a stop and we get out of the vehicle, stretching our arms and legs as we take the picnic basket and blanket out of the back seat. We carry it all down to the shore, and I can't seem to wipe the smile off my face as Breaker lays out the blanket and I begin unpacking the sandwiches and pasta salad I made earlier for this excursion. My stomach rumbles as we sit down to eat, both of us taking deep breaths of the clean, refreshing country air. I've never felt so free, so perfectly content to just exist in the world. With Breaker at my side, everything seems so much brighter, more vivid than ever before.

"The food looks incredible, princess," he tells me honestly, eyeing the sandwiches with obvious hunger. I giggle and pass him one of them, along with a scoop of pasta salad and a fork.

"Is that champagne?" he asks, raising an eyebrow as he looks at the basket.

I snort in amusement and pull out the shiny bottle, holding it up.

"Nope. Sparkling grape juice, sorry," I chuckle.

"Works for me. Besides, looking at how beautiful you are in the sunshine is much more intoxicating than a glass of bubbly," he remarks sweetly.

I blush and look away coyly, picking up my sandwich. We chat and tease each other playfully while we eat, enjoying the warm, sunny day. There's not another soul around for miles and miles, and it's been probably at least an hour since we even passed another car. Out here on the lake, we might as well be on our very own planet, and after the hard times we've faced, it's a massive relief just to be alone together in a lovely location.

"You know, when I think about why I joined that damn club in the first place, it was for all the right reasons. I wanted a community. Friends, family, people to rely on. I wanted to feel like there was somewhere in the world I could truly belong," Breaker says wistfully. Then he turns to give me a passionate smile. "I realize now that I just had to make my own family."

I giggle and wink at him. "Well, with how frequently we've been screwing, that shouldn't be a problem," I tease suggestively.

Breaker laughs and reaches over to hook an arm around me, pulling me in close to kiss me on the lips. A shock of desire rolls through my body. He breaks away to gaze into my eyes.

"With a mouth like that, how can I help myself?" he growls, and I can feel his lust growing for me. I'm getting slick between the thighs for him already, and when he cradles me back onto the blanket and hikes up my dress, I know I'm in for a hell of a ride.

He unzips his jeans and pulls his boxers down just far enough for his cock to spring free, bouncing and stiffening in the fresh air. I bite my lip as he positions the head of his cock at my wet opening, both of us completely ready. These days, it doesn't take much for us to get into the mood. In fact, with him around, I feel like I'm always in the mood. We can't get enough of each other, no matter how many times we fuck.

He slides his cock inside me and we both shudder and moan, clinging to one another. Breaker slides his arms underneath my back and lifts me up, my legs straddling his waist so that we're facing one another. He kisses me and begins to rock his hips, spearing deep inside my clenching pussy until I'm whimpering and gasping for breath.

"Such a dirty little girl, aren't you?" Breaker whispers roughly. "Out here in the middle of nowhere, taking you raw. We could get caught any second now, you know that?"

"Yes, sir," I murmur breathlessly. "I love it."

"That's right, you do," he snarls between gritted teeth.

He picks up the pace, slamming into me as I tilt my head back and close my eyes, feeling his body moving in tandem with mine while the country air wraps me in a blanket of softness. I feel nothing but pleasure and overpowering, overwhelming love for this man. I know without a doubt that my heart has belonged to him ever since the first day we met. Since he rescued me from a fate arguably worse than death. I know, too, that we are going to be together forever. It's destiny. We are made for one another, and now that the world has brought us back together, we'll never let go again. Besides, I trust him more than I've ever trusted anyone. I know I'm perfectly safe in his arms, that he will never do anything to harm me. I can submit to him freely, secure in the understanding that Breaker loves me and will protect me to the death.

His fingers rake through my hair, tangling a

fistful of auburn locks as he tilts my head back further and leans in to nip at my exposed, ticklish neck. I shiver with pleasure, goosebumps rising along my arms and legs as he continues to pound into my slick cunny. We moan each other's names and rock together back and forth, in and out, until finally we're both at the edge.

"Fuck, you feel so good. I'm going to come inside you and make you mine, little girl. Are you ready for that?" he snarls lustfully.

"Yes, sir. Please. Give it to me. I need it," I gasp with desperation.

With one last powerful thrust, the two of us come together, clinging to each other as our bodies shudder and twitch through the powerful climax. We kiss sloppily, our tongues dancing together as his hands slide around to cup my face almost delicately. When he breaks away, he rests his forehead against mine as we try to catch our breath.

He smiles softly and says, "I *told* you I was going to come inside you."

I let out an exhilarated giggle, melting into his strong embrace, and murmur back, "It's just as well. My period is already late—and it's *never* late."

"Alright," I say, standing in the meeting room with three fresh faces standing in front of me, each of them looking different stages of anxious yet determined. "With all that said, you're not the boys you used to be. You're Heartbreakers now, one of us, and don't let anyone tell you otherwise. You've learned our creed, and now I expect you to go live it out. And if you don't, you'll answer to me. Got that?"

"Yes, Prez," the three say almost in unison, and out of the corner of my eye, I can see Bones grinning. He's standing in the room with us, along with the rest of us members who split off from Buzz's gang.

It seemed fitting for all of us to be witnesses to another round of former Buzzsaws prospects getting sworn in to our club.

"Good," I say, cracking a smile. "Now get the fuck

out of here and head upstairs, I'll meet up with the rest of you and ride tonight before we celebrate."

The new members make their way out of the meeting room, leaving me alone with Bones, Ironside, and Big Daddy.

"Another month, another handful of them," Big Daddy chuckles. "Wonder if we'll end up with everyone Buzz rounded up over the years."

"Not everyone," I say, shaking my head. "Some skipped states, and we sure as hell aren't the only two MCs in Wyoming. I don't know if any of them are as sloppy as the Buzzsaws were, but if they are, we'll find them."

"We've almost tripled our numbers in just a few months, so I don't think that's all that unreasonable," Bones agrees, chuckling.

"Think we have anything to worry about from this group?" Ironside muses, scratching his chin thoughtfully and looking up at the map of the area that I've had put back up on the wall. "Buzz is long dead, but I can never help but wonder if his attitude managed to work its way into any of these poor fucks he recruited."

"If it did, it isn't in any of these guys," I say confidently. "Not so far, anyway. I've been vetting all of them personally."

"Don't worry, Prez, we all know that," Ironside says, holding up a hand. "But we need to start keeping eyes and ears out around the club to make sure it stays that way. You won't be able to vet everyone all of the time, if we keep growing at this rate."

"And you're right about that," I agree, nodding slowly. "Good forethought. And on that note, Bones, any word on Diesel?"

Bones shakes his head, frowning, and my jaw tightens. The guy named Diesel was the only face I completely lost track of after the fight at the impound lot. I had the men out looking for him, but he must have gone off on his own and found a good way to lay low. He's a liability I like to keep quiet, because I know all too well what one man can do. And he's one loose end we need brought in, and fast.

"Then you know the drill: make the usual sweeps and leave no stone unturned. If it so much as vaguely looks like a safe house, it's worth looking into. Now, my turn to kick you all out. Go make the new members feel like family, I've got one more piece of business to take care of down here."

"You got it, Prez," Big Daddy says, and the men file out of the room in front of me.

Outside the meeting room, the bar looks better than ever, and it's all thanks to the woman who's currently standing behind the bar, experimenting with a cocktail as the guys walk past her and give her respectful nods or brief greetings. I take my seat at the end of the bar as Kate watches the last of the guys leave, and she slowly makes her way around the bar.

And as soon as she emerges, I can't help but smile at the bump on her belly. The look of excitement on her face when she first told me is going to be emblazoned in my mind forever as a happy memory to go back to, just like every day with Kate at my side has been.

"Hey, good lookin'," I say casually, leaning on the bar with a wolfish grin. "Teasing yourself with drinks you can't have yet?"

"You gave me a bottomless budget to flip this little speakeasy you've got running," she says with a smirk, "so yeah, I'm gonna make sure it has some fancy drinks to go with it. It'll be something to surprise Eli with when he gets in later."

"Let me know if he ever tries to steal credit, I'll pop his ass," I chuckle, completely joking. Ever since we recruited the old bartender from Buzz's operation, he's been an endlessly grateful friend to us. Seems like Buzz didn't get any better to work for with time.

Kate really had done a fantastic job with the bar, and she's seamlessly slipped into the role of manager around here. There were new lights hanging from the ceilings, the wood was all restored, we'd gotten new barstools that matched the stained glass of the lights, and the whole space didn't reek of tobacco and cheap whisky anymore.

That alone would have been an accomplishment in and of itself.

She's gone so far out of her way for me, so I treat her like the queen she is. I get her anything in my power that she wants, and right now, I've got a lot of power to share. She's become like an advisor to me in a lot of ways, and her advice is always worth listening to. Her instincts on problem prospects are always right, she has good business sense, and there aren't any more secrets between us. She has become the best friend I always feel like I have to improve myself for, and without her, the MC simply wouldn't exist.

I make that known to every prospect who comes through our doors, from day one.

Well, alright, I wasn't entirely honest. There is *something* she doesn't know just yet, but that's all about to change.

"So, is that all the club business you've got tonight?" she asks, sitting down on the barstool next to me and leaning back with a warm smile.

"I don't know, do you count as club business?" I ask, grinning and leaning in to kiss her. She giggles as I pepper her face with kisses across her cheek and down her neck. She tries to squirm away, and we laugh as I wrap my arms around her and tickle her with the scruff on my face.

"Maybe I should," she says as we settle down and meet each other's loving gaze.

"You know," I say, "knowing it'll be just you and me at the end of the day, nothing but us-time, even if we don't have time to fool around… that's what keeps me going."

Her smile gently grows into a grin as color comes to her cheeks, and she turns her gaze away and covers her mouth. "Oh my god, don't make me blush right before we go out and see everyone," she laughs.

"It's true though," I say with a big, stupid grin on my face, taking her hand and brushing her hair out of her eyes. She looks up at me, and any anxious nerves I had before now settle down. "You're an angel I don't deserve, sweetheart, but if you're crazy enough to ride with me… I want to make it official."

Somehow as smoothly as I practiced endlessly in my room, I reach into my kutte's pocket and take out the ring box, then get out of my seat and get down onto a knee as Kate's face flushes, and she lowers her hands from her mouth to beam at me.

"Kate-" I say, fighting back a tear in my eye, but Kate calmly puts a hand over the ring box. My smile vanishes, and my heart stops for a moment as she holds it shut and peers down at me. Did I just make the biggest mistake of the year without a second thought?

"Damien Brooks," she says, making my mouth fall open. I've never told anyone my real name, not even Kate yet. I had been planning to do that at this exact moment. "I'll be more than happy to marry you, and while I'm at it, I *love* the house up the road you just bought us."

I know I've been a man who can run his mouth, so I can't say I've ever been stunned to silence in my life. But Kate has just done exactly that, so I'll never be able to say it's impossible. My thoughts come to a screeching halt and start to short-circuit as I stare up at her slack jawed, and she finally bursts into laughter, pulling me up to my feet by the hand, throwing her arms around me, and kissing me on my open mouth.

Her kiss is so warm that I'm almost distracted, but she breaks it a moment later and smiles up at me lovingly.

"I don't think you know how perfect you made that," she says with a satisfied sigh. "Since you took so many liberties digging through my life, I thought I'd return the favor and dig through yours. I found the ring last month, and I found the paperwork for the home sale last week, which had your legal name on it," she explains, looking so unbelievably smug that I can't help but feel my heart bursting with love for her.

"You… sure are proud of that one, aren't you, sweetheart?" I said as I hugged her to me, running my hand through her hair, still laughing as a tear of joy rolls down my face. "There's nobody else in the world I'd rather spend my life with. You've just made me the happiest man alive. Don't you ever change."

"Don't think I'm not going to cry too, though," she adds through sniffling, and I break the hug to kiss her forehead as she laugh-sobs once and clasps my hands. "But… I do have a question for you, now."

"I'm all ears, sugar," I chuckle.

"If we have a wedding, would you like to invite your mom?"

My eyes widen, and I wipe the wetness from them before blinking at her in surprise.

"When I found the ring, I thought you might like that," she says with a sheepish smile. "So… I know this is a little more sensitive than knowing about the house, but I tracked your mom down, too."

She takes out her phone and swipes through the screen for a moment, and my phone buzzes.

"And now you've got her number," she finishes as I feel a lump in my throat. "So, the decision is totally yours, but I'll support whatever you decide."

"Oh honey," I say, and I hug her again, feeling my heart thumping hard against my chest. "I… I don't know what to say. Thank you. I… yeah, I think I'd like her there, if she wants to be there. And yeah, shit yeah we're having a wedding!"

I break the hug and grin at her, not hiding the tears in my eyes any more than she is in hers.

"And we'll invite your whole family too, have them on one side and the club on the other. Cake, honeymoon, flowers, a suit, I'm going all the way."

"Even a suit?" Kate asks, laughing by now and

wiping a tear from her eye. "I never thought I'd see that, but now you've got me too curious to back down."

"Alright, just one condition on that," I add, holding up a hand.

"What's that?" she asks playfully.

"I get to wear my kutte with the suit," I say, grinning.

Kate giggles, and she puts her hands on my kutte to pull herself up to my face and kiss me.

"Breaker," she says, "I wouldn't have it any other way."

~

Thank you so much for reading! I hope you enjoyed <3 If you have a moment, please leave a review. Other readers are dying to know what you thought.

I hope you're ready for more of the Heart-breakers MC, as Bones, Ironside and Big Daddy all need their own story, coming in 2019! While you wait, make sure you check out my other books on the next couple of pages, and sign up for my newsletter to be notified when I have a new release on the way!

~Alexis Abbott

Trafficked

Stealing Her

The Assassin's Heart

Killing For Her

Abducted

Killers:

Hunter's Baby

I Hired A Hitman

Stepbrothers:

Ruthless

Criminal

Glitz & Grit:

Betting on Love

Vegas Boss

Rock Hard Bodyguard

Innocence For Sale: Jane

Redeeming Viktor

Sexy SEALs

Sweetheart for the SEAL

Sights on the SEAL

<u>Romance:</u>

Falling for her Boss (Novella)

Most Wanted: Lilly (Novella)

Bound as the World Burns (SFF)

ABOUT THE AUTHOR

Alexis Abbott is a Wall Street Journal & USA Today bestselling author who writes about bad boys protecting their girls! Pick up her books today if you can't resist a bad boy who is a good man, and find yourself transported with super steamy sex, gritty suspense, and lots of romance.

She lives in beautiful St. John's, NL, Canada with her amazing husband.

facebook.com/abbottauthor

twitter.com/abbottauthor

instagram.com/alexisabbottauthor

bookbub.com/authors/alexis-abbott

pinterest.com/badboyromance

youtube.com/AlexisAbbott

ACKNOWLEDGMENTS

Thank you to my amazing Patrons. I'm constantly humbled and grateful for your support.

Ramona Cabrera
Melissa Hedrick
Virginia Swanson
Dawn Daughenbaugh
Don Doss
Stacie Currie

If you'd like to join them — and get my ebooks or paperbacks — you can find me here on Patreon.
https://www.patreon.com/alexisabbott